The Fledglings

The Fledglings
Sandra Markle

BANTAM BOOKS
NEW YORK • TORONTO • LONDON • SYDNEY • AUCKLAND

The author wishes to express her special thanks to Reverend Robert H. Bushyhead for sharing his expert knowledge of the North Carolina dialect of the Cherokee language.

THE FLEDGLINGS

A Bantam Book / June 1992

The Starfire logo is a registered trademark of Bantam Books, a division of Bantam Doubleday Dell Publishing Group, Inc. Registered in U.S. Patent and Trademark Office and elsewhere.

LIBRARY OF CONGRESS CATALOGING-IN-PUBLICATION DATA
Markle, Sandra.
The fledglings / Sandra Markle.
p.   cm.
Summary: Orphaned after the death of her mother, fourteen-year-old Kate runs away to live with her grandfather, a Cherokee Indian who is trying to stop the poaching of predator birds.
ISBN 0-553-07729-5
[1. Grandfathers—Fiction.   2. Cherokee Indians—Fiction.
3. Indians of North America—Fiction.   4. Birds—Fiction.
5. North Carolina—Fiction.]   I. Title.
PZ7.M3396F1   1992
[Fic]—dc20   91-36017
CIP
AC

Published simultaneously in the United States and Canada

Bantam Books are published by Bantam Books, a division of Bantam Doubleday Dell Publishing Group, Inc. Its trademark, consisting of the words "Bantam Books" and the portrayal of a rooster, is Registered in U.S. Patent and Trademark Office and in other countries. Marca Registrada. Bantam Books, 666 Fifth Avenue, New York, New York 10103.

PRINTED IN THE UNITED STATES OF AMERICA

BVG   0 9 8 7 6 5 4 3 2 1

For Dorothy Markinko who gives
wings to my dreams

The Fledglings

One

I jerked to a stop, looking in the direction of the crackling sound I'd heard. Only shadows lurked between the
tall trees, but I still had the creepy feeling that I was
being watched. I swung around, scanning the woods. No
one was there. All I could see were tall trees. Shrubs
edged the forest, and the rutted red-clay path I was following was sprinkled with red, yellow, and purple wildflowers. Beyond the forest were the hazy, blue-green,
round-topped mountains—layer upon layer of them. Gazing out upon so much wilderness, I felt homesick for the
familiar stone-and-glass peaks of the downtown Atlanta
skyline. What in the world was I doing out here all by
myself in the North Carolina mountains?

I wiped sweat from my forehead and considered—for
the umpteenth time—turning around and going back to
Atlanta. Then, once again, I decided that I wasn't going
back. If my aunt Mildred caught me, she was going to

kill me for running away! No, I wasn't going back. I was going to do what I'd set out to do—and that was to find my grandfather.

I don't even know what he looks like, I thought, as I started walking again. Until yesterday, I'd thought he was dead. That was what Mom had told me. I wondered again what the big mystery was, what he had done or what had happened that had made Mom decide to keep him a secret from me all these years. And me from him.

Suddenly, there was another crackling noise among the trees, and I jerked to a stop, swiveling in the direction of the sound.

It's only the wind. Stop imagining things. I took a deep breath—

Crack! That was definitely more than the wind moving through the trees. Another crackling noise followed, and this time I caught a glimpse of a shape slipping between shadows.

For a few long, horrible seconds I froze, staring at the spot where the creature had passed, and a shiver rippled through me despite the heat. It was a gray-brown animal the size of a large dog. Was it really a dog that I'd seen? Or was it something else—like a bear. But it was the wrong shape to be a bear. *A wolf?* Were there wolves in the North Carolina mountains?

I pinched my lower lip between my teeth, worrying. *What should I do now? Should I go back down the mountain?*

I'd already been walking up this trail a very long time without passing any houses or even any other people. That meant that it would take a very long time to get back to Cherokee and to find help. Besides, going in that direction would mean heading directly toward whatever was following me.

Following me?

"Ohhh," I moaned, and started walking up the mountain again—faster this time. The fatigue that had been making my feet drag was forgotten now. I gripped the duffel's shoulder strap and tried to keep the heavy bag from slamming into my side.

Snap. I jerked my head toward the sound and caught another glimpse of the animal. I wanted to run, but I was afraid that might make it bolt after me, so I just kept walking as fast as I could.

Two more times, I heard the rustling noise and caught glimpses of the wild animal. *The beast must be stalking me*, I thought, feeling panic start to rise.

Since it was July, I knew it wasn't going to be really dark for hours, but I suspected the sun would sink into twilight behind the mountains much faster here than it did back home in Atlanta. I definitely didn't want to be caught up here in the mountains at night—alone. I didn't want to be here even when it got to be twilight—alone. In fact, I wasn't too happy about being here alone right this minute.

I finally decided that I would keep walking and looking for the fork in the road for another ten minutes. If I hadn't come to the fork by then, I'd turn back.

Five minutes later I reached the fork in the road, and I took the path to the right feeling both happy and dismayed. I was happy because reaching this point on the trail meant I was getting close to my grandfather's house. I was dismayed, though, because this trail immediately became more winding and narrow. Then, abruptly, it seemed to just end. I'd followed it into a grove of tall skinny pines and then lost it. If the trail actually did continue through the woods, it was completely buried under a thick carpet of dry pine needles. All I could do was keep on walking, hoping the trail would pick up again when I reached the grassy meadow up ahead.

I was nearly there when I heard a twig snap to my left. This time I saw the animal clearly. It was a huge German shepherd. The dog stopped too, and we stared at each other across the quiet, deeply shadowed woods for seconds that seemed like hours. Then the dog growled a low rumbling thunder that shuddered through me.

I was horrified. That wasn't a wolf, but the German shepherd looked and sounded wild. I kept my eyes on the animal as if that might help hold it at bay and began to back away in the direction of the clearing. If I could reach it, I'd be in the open, where I could run without the risk of tripping over a root or slipping on the dry pine needles.

I kept moving, but each time I took a step, the German shepherd advanced too. Without waiting any longer, I swung toward the grassy meadow and ran. For the first couple of sprinting steps the duffel bag slammed into my ribs. Then I shrugged off the strap, and as the heavy weight of the bag dropped off my shoulder I was able to run faster.

I slipped twice on the slick pine-needle carpet, but I didn't fall. When I reached the meadow, the going was easier. I didn't look for the trail—didn't care about finding it. All I wanted to do was get away from the big dog. I glanced over my shoulder and saw the German shepherd burst out of the woods and charge across the grass still intent on running me down.

I should have climbed a tree, I thought. That was what I was going to have to do now. I saw one ahead with branches low enough for me to reach easily. I ran to it and climbed up quickly.

The dog charged after me, barking and hurling himself up the trunk in an attempt to reach me. I climbed higher and higher until, at last, I was safely out of reach. I clung to my perch and looked down at the dog. He was sitting on his haunches, watching me.

What am I doing out here on this mountain alone? I wondered again. Until yesterday, I would never have dreamed of coming to a wilderness area like this by myself. For that matter, until a few days ago, I would never have dreamed of running away. My whole life had changed in just a few days.

Two

As I continued to watch the German shepherd, I thought about yesterday afternoon, not the funeral, but the gathering at our house afterward. It had been there that I'd learned the secret my mother had kept from me my whole life, and that was the reason I was here now.

I remembered how I'd come out of the kitchen, carrying a tray loaded with little sandwiches, and Mrs. Roskowski had surprised me by plucking it from my hands. "Oh dear, you don't need to do that," she said.

I wanted to tell her I *did* need to carry that tray. It had given me something to do besides listen to people or, worse, think. I couldn't stand thinking about what the people were saying. Why they were here. The funeral had been so few hours ago.

I'd been seriously tempted to snatch the tray back. But, of course, I hadn't. That would have been rude, and Mrs. Roskowski was just trying to be kind. At the rate my elderly neighbor was pushing the bite-size sandwiches into her mouth, the tray was likely to be empty soon anyway.

"You poor darling," Mrs. Roskowski crooned between swallows. Tears welled up along the rims of her large dark brown eyes and threatened to spill over onto her cheeks. "Dan and I feel so awful about this. It's such a terrible—totally dreadful—thing. Your poor, sweet mother."

Mrs. Roskowski patted my cheek with the hand that had been propelling the sandwiches into her mouth, and her touch left my skin feeling sticky and moist. "If only Dan and I were younger," she announced, "*we'd* offer to take care of you. We never had any children, and we've always been so fond of you, Kate.

"We used to babysit for you sometimes, you know." She smiled, with her lower lip trembling. Then she added, "Thank heavens for your mother's sister. I know it'll be hard for you to leave your home and your friends, but you're young. You'll adjust. And you'll be with *family*. It's the best thing for you."

Mrs. Roskowski patted my cheek again, selected one more sandwich from the tray, and deposited it in her mouth. Then she walked into the living room with a rolling gait, and I headed back toward the kitchen, seeking a new gimmick to appear occupied.

Living with Mr. and Mrs. Roskowski—the thought of it was scary, but not as scary as living with my aunt Mildred. As if on cue, my two cousins burst out of my bedroom, fighting over something—something of mine. I didn't want to guess what. Their normally loud, shrill voices were even louder and higher-pitched in combat. They flew down the hall, coming straight at me. With their short, blond hair bobbing around their pinched faces, they reminded me of the two Siamese cats in *Lady and the Tramp.*

At least they weren't looking for me. They stormed through the swinging kitchen door, yelling for their mother. Josie, eight and the older of the two, was in the lead. Becca, six and close on her heels, was bellowing plaintively in an obvious attempt to appear the injured party in whatever claim was about to be made.

I didn't want to know the details, and I didn't want to be around for the outcome, because I'd probably get stuck *helping*, which meant trying to control those two, and that was an impossible task. I slipped around the corner into the living room and pushed my way into a small vacant space behind the wing chair that faced the fireplace. I was hoping to go unnoticed. I didn't really believe I'd be able to escape for long, though. Aunt Mildred, who always seemed overwhelmed by her two daughters, was even more so now that she was eight months pregnant. She was constantly looking for somebody to take them off her hands, and that somebody had become me. Uncle Frank was always either too busy or too tired, or simply nowhere to be found. He was very good at making himself unavailable.

The Josie and Becca storm raged louder. Even the noise of the air conditioner grinding against the afternoon heat and the chatter of people talking didn't drown them out. Their voices rose so loud and shrill that some of the people in the living room stopped talking and turned, looking in the direction of the kitchen. It would be only a matter of moments before Aunt Mildred called for me.

I felt trapped, desperate to escape. It had been one

thing to have to "play" with the girls when we went to visit Mom's sister during the summer or on holidays. Now I sensed that this responsibility was going to be my daily duty in return for being given a home. I would even have to share a room with those two once I left Atlanta and went to live with them in Toledo, Ohio.

I had this recurring flash daydream of being tied to the clothesline pole in my aunt and uncle's backyard with lots of dried leaves heaped around my feet. Josie and Becca were fighting over who was going to light the bonfire.

I looked at the picture of Mom smiling at me from its familiar place on the fireplace mantel and felt suddenly angry. Very angry. Terribly, completely angry—at her.

How dare you smile at me, I thought. *Look what you're doing to me.*

Then just as quickly, the anger was gone, and I felt sad, guilty, ashamed. It wasn't her fault that some drunk driver had smashed into her car while she was on the way to the grocery store. Mom didn't want to be dead.

I knew she hadn't left me on purpose, but knowing that didn't help. I felt abandoned. Tears were burning my eyes and threatening to pour out again if I let them. Only, I wasn't going to let them. Not now. I blinked the tears away and swallowed, fighting the feeling that threatened to produce more tears. I wasn't going to have all these people feeling sorry for me because I'd lost my mother, even though my mother was all I had. It was so unfair.

"Hi, Kate." I jumped a little. I was surprised to have someone talk to me when I was feeling so alone. Then I realized it was my best friend, Chrissy Weber.

"Hey. You okay?"

"No," I said. Chrissy and I always told each other the truth. We'd been best friends since Mrs. Stelten's class for four-year-olds at the Cross and Crown Preschool.

We had everything in common. We both liked swimming and art and hot fudge sundaes. We both hated social studies, particularly map skills, and thought Kirk Cameron and Mr. Farwell, the physical education teacher, were totally *RAD*. We shared everything too, from lunches and a crush on Tommy McAffin to chicken pox, working on Girl Scout merit badges, and producing a winning science project on garbage last year in the seventh grade. We were more like sisters than friends, and one of the really special bonds we felt for each other was that we each had only a mother.

Actually, Chrissy had a dad, too, but her parents were divorced. Since her dad lived in California and she spent only three weeks every summer with him, we never counted him. He did count, though. If anything happened to Chrissy's mother, she'd still have her dad. My father had been killed when I was still a baby, in the war everybody called 'Nam. I couldn't remember anything about him, so I felt like I never had a dad.

Chrissy wrinkled her nose in disgust as she listened to the commotion coming from the kitchen. "Those two are too much. Don't they ever stop?"

"Never!" I answered.

"They would if your mom ..." Chrissy started. Then she stopped and quickly looked down at her skirt, as if she'd spotted a bug on it. I could tell her cheeks were pink. She seemed really embarrassed, as if she'd said something she'd been told not to. And she stood there not talking.

So I didn't say anything either. We both just stood

there not talking for the longest time. But I was thinking that I knew what Chrissy had been about to say. If Mom were here, Josie and Becca wouldn't be fighting. Mom would have found something wonderful for all of us to do and everybody would have been too busy having fun to argue.

Mom was like that. She was great with kids because she was a teacher. Or maybe she had become a teacher because she was great with kids. I'd never really thought about it. I'd always just taken it for granted. Like I'd always taken it for granted that she and I would be together forever. Even after I was grown up, I figured Mom and I would still be friends. We were such good friends, Mom and I.

My throat was feeling tight again. "I'd better go to the kitchen and help Aunt Mildred," I said.

"Yeah. Okay," Chrissy said, still looking uncomfortable.

I maneuvered along the edge of the living room close to the wall because it was easier than pushing through the groups of people packing the middle of the room. Our little house was bulging. There were teachers Mom had worked with, parents of students she'd had in school the past ten years, and even some of her old students. Most of her adult Sunday school class was also here, along with many of our neighbors. I hadn't realized Mom knew so many people, but then we'd lived in the same house in the same neighborhood in Dunwoody, a suburb on the north side of Atlanta, forever. Mom and Dad had bought this house before I was born. When Dad was killed in the war, the insurance paid off the mortgage. Now, Mr. Wescott, Mom's lawyer, told me the house was mine, only, he called it my future. The house was going to be sold—along with almost everything in it—and the money put into a trust fund for me. This house and some certificates of deposit Mom left were supposed to pay Aunt Mildred for my support and pay for my college education in four years.

Four years. Four years of living with Aunt Mildred and Uncle Frank and Josie and Becca and whoever the new baby was. It seemed like a life sentence.

I was about to excuse myself to the group of people blocking my exit into the hall. But before I could get anyone's attention I heard my name, so I stood still and listened.

"Reverend Maxwell went to such a lot of effort to track him down too." It was Mrs. Harris, the church secretary, who was speaking. "I couldn't hear the man's end of the conversation," she continued, "but I could certainly hear Reverend Maxwell. And the Reverend told him most emphatically that it was his responsibility as her grandfather to provide a home for Kate now that both her mother and father were dead."

"Yes, a grandfather that could give her the love and attention she needs right now would be wonderful for Kate," Mrs. Jenson, our other next-door neighbor, said. "I mean, the sister seems like a good soul, but she certainly has her hands full with her own children."

"But he wouldn't take the child?" This from Mrs. Wuertenberg, a lady in Mom's Sunday school class.

"No. Wouldn't even consider it," Mrs. Harris confirmed. "I could tell that much from how put out Reverend Maxwell was."

"I didn't think Susan had any other family left." I wasn't sure who had raised that question, but I was glad she had. It was exactly what I was thinking. Mom's parents were both dead, her mother long ago, before any history I could remember, and Grandpa two years ago this fall.

"Oh, not *her* father," Mrs. Harris explained. "Her fa-ther-*in-law*."

Judging from the sounds the other women in the group made, they were as stunned as I by this revelation.

"All these years and the man's never done anything for his son's family. Never been to see his grandchild."

"Maybe Susan wouldn't let him. Maybe this was the way she wanted it."

"Oh, no. I'll never believe that," Mrs. Harris insisted. "Susan was always so loving. Knowing her, I can imagine she would have insisted on raising her child on her own. But I can't believe she wouldn't have wanted Kate to know her own grandfather, wouldn't have made an effort to share family holidays with him. At least Christmases."

"Well. I don't think they ever did."

"No. I'm sure they never did."

Never, I thought.

"Whatever the past, I can't believe, under the circum-stances, that the man wouldn't want to help his son's child now," Mrs. Wuertenberg said.

"The man didn't seem to believe Kate was his grandchild."

"Well, didn't Reverend Maxwell set him straight on that?"

"He tried," Mrs. Harris explained. "But the man hung up, and by the time Reverend Maxwell could put a call through again, the man had already left."

"Left?"

"Yes. He doesn't have a telephone. That's why he was so very hard to reach, even after Reverend Maxwell found out about him from the Veterans Administration.

And after he hung up, no one could get him to come back to the phone."

"How awful!"

"Where in the world does this man live?" Mrs. Wuertenberg demanded. "Somewhere remote? Out west?"

"No. He's not so very far away actually," Mrs. Harris told them. "I put the original call through. Susan's father-in-law lives up in the Blue Ridge Mountains of North Carolina outside of Cherokee. It's only about a four-hour drive from here. That's why I found it so amazing that they hadn't gotten together in all these years."

Mrs. Harris and the others moved into the hall then, and their voices trailed off. But it didn't matter. I'd heard enough.

For whatever reasons, I'd never met him, but my father's father was alive. I had a grandfather.

Three

I watched hopefully as the German shepherd ambled away, seemingly no longer interested in me. When the dog didn't return, I decided this was my chance to escape, and I began to climb down. Just as I reached the lowest limb, the big dog rushed back, barking.

Panic surged through me again as the dog leapt. Its sharp teeth nipped the heel of my sneaker. I frantically reached for the limb above me and hauled myself up, climbing until I was once again safely out of reach. That had been close—too close.

I regretted again coming to this wild place on my own, but I reasoned that I hadn't really had a choice. Aunt Mildred never would have brought me to Cherokee or helped me to find my grandfather. It was something I knew I'd have to do myself, and I decided that afternoon after the funeral that I'd run away.

•   •   •

I was eager to tell Chrissy the amazing news I'd over-heard, and we went to my room to be alone. I stopped in the doorway to my bedroom, staring in stunned disbelief. It was a disaster. Josie and Becca had been rummaging through my old dolls and games. Their own toys and clothes were also scattered everywhere, and the roll-away bed—still unmade—was pushed against the closet door just beyond the end of my big four-poster bed. Seeing my beautiful room like this—the room Mom and I had worked so hard to decorate—made me sick.

"I've got to get out of here," I said suddenly. I only meant to tell Chrissy I had a grandfather, but now an unexpected inspiration swept over me.

"It's really a mess," Chrissy said. "Why don't we go out on the solarium if it isn't too hot or crowded."

"No." I told her. "I've got to get away from them: Aunt Mildred, Josie, Becca—all of them."

Chrissy's expression was compassionate. "But where can you go? You told me the lawyer said it was in your mom's will that you're supposed to live with them. And besides, where else could you live?" Chrissy paused, then added, "I asked my mom if you could live with us. She likes you a lot, but she said it just wasn't possible."

"I didn't know you asked your mom." I was touched at what a good friend Chrissy was.

"Wouldn't you do the same thing for me?"

I admitted that I would.

"I don't think your aunt would let you move in with us anyway," Chrissy added. "I think she really wants the money she's going to get for keeping you, plus, you'd be a good helper with the kids. It looks like you're stuck living with her."

I took a deep breath and said, "No. I'm going to my grandfather's."

Chrissy's look was of sheer disbelief. "He's dead."

"Not my grandpa Evans," I told her. Then I went on to explain the conversation I'd overheard.

Chrissy swept the spilled contents of several board games out of the way and flopped onto my bed. "C'mon, get real," she said. "You can't run away. I think it's against the law until you're eighteen, or at least sixteen. Besides, what good is it going to do you to find him? I mean, the man told a minister he didn't want anything to do with you."

These arguments were more practical than I was prepared to be at this moment. I was desperate, drowning. I felt so alone now that Mom was gone. I didn't believe I would ever really fit in as part of my aunt's family. We didn't like any of the same things, not even the same foods. And Aunt Mildred didn't believe in trying anything new. She was totally the opposite of my mom. I remembered the time Mom and I went on a terrific white-water canoe trip. Aunt Mildred freaked out. She said it was crazy and that she couldn't believe Mom and I risked our lives that way.

She didn't see things the way Mom and I did, and I didn't think I could stand knowing that the next four years were going to be completely boring. This was my only chance to be rescued. Besides, I couldn't go off to Toledo without finding out what my grandfather was like, and why Mom had kept him from me—and me from him—all these years. "He doesn't *know* I'm his grand-daughter," I insisted. "Mrs. Harris said that, remember. Reverend Maxwell was trying to convince him when he hung up."

"Yeah, he *hung up*." Chrissy shook a finger in the air. "There's got to be some reason he did that. Maybe he doesn't want anything to do with a kid, or he's a really mean and grumpy person. Maybe he's got something to hide and he doesn't want anybody—especially the law— to have a reason to poke around in his business. Maybe he runs drugs. Maybe he raises marijuana and sells it."

"Give me a break, Chrissy." I pushed more junk out of the way and sat down on the bed too.

"You're just letting your curiosity get the best of you again. Remember the time you *had* to find out why the Roskowskis had all their basement windows painted black?"

"You were curious too. And we only got in trouble because the window broke when we tried to scrape the paint off so we could peek inside. Who would have figured Mrs. Roskowski had taken up photography and put a darkroom in the basement? Besides, this is different. It's more than curiosity this time. I want to get to know my grandfather."

"But did you ever hear anything about this grandfather before?" Chrissy demanded. "Have you ever seen a picture of him?"

"I only know his name," I admitted. "But what does that prove?"

"Well, there has to be some explanation for why your mom never took you to see him. She even told you he was dead."

"Maybe they had a terrible fight a long time ago," I suggested. "That happens sometimes. Years and years slip by and nobody ever gets around to saying they're sorry. So they don't make up. Then it's too late. Like now."

"Okay," Chrissy conceded, "let's say it was like that. Let's even say that he'd want to get to know you if he knew you were alive. But he doesn't. How are you going to convince him you're his granddaughter? How are you going to get in touch with him? You can't even call him up."

"Then I'll just have to go and see him," I announced. "When I explain to him . . ."

"You don't know where he lives, do you?"

"Well, I do—sorta."

"No, you don't. You only know he lives somewhere outside of Cherokee, North Carolina, in the mountains. That could be *anywhere*. Kate, he doesn't even have a phone. This Cherokee place must be pretty wild country."

Chrissy had a point, and it made me hesitate. But only for a minute. "Somebody got him to come to a phone so Reverend Maxwell could talk to him," I persisted. "So that means people in the area know where he lives. And if they can find him, I can find him."

"You're serious, aren't you?" Chrissy said quietly. Then she added, "Oh, Kate, you shouldn't have told me. You know I'm awful about keeping secrets. Mom'll probably get it out of me, then she'll tell your aunt and uncle, and they'll go get you."

I smiled suddenly at my best friend, my almost sister. I loved her so much. I rocked forward and hugged her, and she hugged me back. "You're not going to tell anyone this secret," I assured her. "It's too important. You can do it."

"I'll try," Chrissy promised. "But they're bound to figure it out eventually."

"I know, but if I can convince him I'm his granddaughter, maybe he'll let me stay with him for the summer.

And if the lawyers or a judge or whoever handles guardianship cases know that my grandfather wants me, maybe they'll let me live with him. Then it won't matter if my aunt and uncle find me."

There were an awful lot of ifs in what I'd just said. Big ifs. There were even more ifs than the ones I'd said. I still didn't know what kind of person my grandfather was. There had to be some reason my mother had kept his existence a secret from me. But, then, she'd also kept my existence a secret from him. It was all a big mystery.

"And you'll write to me?" Chrissy asked.

"As soon as it's safe to," I promised. "And when everything's settled, you'll come visit. Cherokee is a lot closer than Toledo, Ohio."

"How are you going to get there?" Chrissy wondered aloud.

"I guess by bus. I won't have enough money for a plane ticket even if there is an airport in Cherokee."

"Are you sure you have enough for the bus?"

The door opened then, and Becca stuck her head into the room. "Mama's looking for you," she reported.

My heart leapt. I hoped desperately that my little cousin hadn't been listening outside the door. Then I consoled myself with the knowledge that Becca was never quiet long enough to be sneaky.

"Tell her I'll be there in a minute," I said, forcing myself to smile sweetly.

"No. Mama wants you to come right *now.*"

"In a minute," I repeated, and then added in a still gentle but more forceful tone, "Go and tell her, Becca."

"Mama's gonna be mad at you for not coming. Really

m-a-d." Becca scrunched her face up as she relayed this information, but then, mercifully, she left.

As soon as the door closed, I slid my desk chair over to the door, wedging the top edge of the back under the handle. I wanted to buy myself some time in case Becca came back—or worse, returned with her sister or mother. Thank heavens Mom had given me my own phone for my fourteenth birthday. "Get the phone book," I ordered. "It's in the bottom drawer of my nightstand. Find the Trailways number."

Chrissy tugged the fat phone book onto the bed and began thumbing through it. After a few moments, she reported, "I've got it."

I dialed as she read me the number, then used my lower, grown-up voice to ask for the bus information. "There's a bus tonight at six and one tomorrow morning at seven-fifteen," I repeated to Chrissy. "The ticket costs fifty-two dollars and forty-nine cents."

"One way?" Chrissy sounded shocked.

"No, round trip, silly. I have to buy a round-trip ticket. A kid buying a one-way ticket would be sure to attract attention." What I didn't admit was that I liked the idea of having a return bus ticket. Just in case.

"I guess getting a round-trip ticket is smart," Chrissy agreed. "But have you got that much money?"

"Yes and no. I've only got eleven dollars of my own. But I know where Mom always keeps some emergency money stashed in the linen closet under the towels. I'll bet there's enough there to make up the difference."

"Let's find out," Chrissy said.

The linen closet was in the hall opposite the bathroom, next to the room that had been my mother's. Aunt

Mildred and Uncle Frank were using her room while they were here. The door to the bedroom was half open, and I could see Uncle Frank stretched out on the bed reading the newspaper. Now I knew why he wasn't around to help with Josie and Becca.

Chrissy and I exchanged cautioning looks, then we tiptoed very quietly to the linen closet.

"Watch him," I whispered. Chrissy nodded, leaning back enough to see around the door. I began to feel under the stacks of towels for the small leather wallet I knew was there.

I tried three stacks with no luck. Maybe Mom had moved the emergency fund without telling me. Or maybe Aunt Mildred had discovered this secret while getting towels for the girls' bath. I heard newspaper rustling and froze. I looked at Chrissy.

"It's okay," she whispered. "He's just turning the page."

I took a deep breath and began to feel around again. Finally, I found what I was looking for in the middle of a stack of hand towels. I pulled out the worn brown leather wallet that had my father's initials, MJR, embossed on the front. Inside, there was a twenty, a five, and a one. My heart sank as I added up the grand total.

"Enough?" Chrissy asked softly.

I shook my head. "Sixteen dollars short." It might as well have been a million. Just then my aunt Mildred called me again, and I looked up, startled, to see her coming down the hall.

"What are you doing?" she demanded. "I sent Becca to tell you I needed you."

"Uh ... Well ... I," I stammered.

"We were getting fresh towels for the bathrooms, Mrs.

Linsley," Chrissy explained in a rush. "We learned in health class how important it is for people to dry their hands on clean towels when they go to the bathroom. It's good hygiene."

I took advantage of the moment to push the bills and wallet back under the stack of towels. Then I lifted out the whole stack and turned to face my aunt.

"Well, I don't think we need soil every towel in the house for strangers. I'm planning to box the towels to take home with me." Aunt Mildred gently stroked the top of her bulging stomach. "Kate, I need you to entertain the girls for a while. They're just too much for me today, what with all these strangers around."

I wanted to say that these weren't *strangers*. They were all my mother's friends. *And* these were my mother's towels. But I didn't say anything because I knew Aunt Mildred wouldn't understand. She was one of those adults who saw things only from her own point of view.

"I'll be glad to watch Josie and Becca for you, Mrs. Linsley," Chrissy offered. "Kate needs to pack. She's going to spend the night with me."

"She is?" Aunt Mildred looked surprised.

I felt surprised too. Chrissy didn't understand that I no longer needed a cover, at least not until I had enough money for the bus ticket.

"My mother thought it would make things easier for your family to have the house to yourselves tonight," Chrissy continued. "It's been such an exhausting day. And when we bring Kate back in the morning, we'll stay to help you pack."

"How thoughtful of your mother," Aunt Mildred crooned.

As I listened to the two of them discuss the details of

my going to Chrissy's house for the night my brain slowly began to function again. Sixteen dollars wasn't an impossible sum. There had to be a way to get the money I needed. It would definitely be a lot easier to get away from Chrissy's house than to slip out of the bed I was sharing with Josie and escape from here. I just needed to think of a way to come up with the money.

Four

In the end, getting the money had been amazingly easy. Mrs. Roskowski pressed a crisp five dollar bill into my hand as she was leaving. She told me it was for my trip, but I didn't tell her how appropriate that was. Unfortunately, Chrissy had recently gone on a shopping spree, but she gladly gave me the seven dollars she had left. I needed only another four dollars, though I realized I should have a little extra money just in case.

As much as we hated to do it, Chrissy and I slipped into the kitchen after her Mom was asleep and took twenty dollars out of her mother's purse. I felt awful about it, but Chrissy convinced me it was okay. I left a note in the wallet:

> Dear Mrs. Weber,
>   I'm sorry for taking twenty dollars. I figured you'd understand. I promise to pay you back as soon as I can.
> Love, Kate

Before Chrissy's mom got up the next morning, I'd slipped out of the house and had taken the train downtown to the Trailways bus station. Getting to Cherokee had been relatively easy compared to everything that had happened since I'd arrived. I looked down at the dog, and it growled threateningly.

I probably would have been better off taking the next bus back to Atlanta, I thought. I'd almost done just that after walking through Cherokee.

The town's main street was a long strip of single-story buildings that looked like something from the Old West or at least a Western movie. There were totem poles in front of a couple of the stores, and several "warriors" and "squaws" in traditional Indian costumes were standing behind tables of merchandise set up on the sidewalk. One young man in leggings with a colorful breechcloth, feathered arm bands, a lavish headdress, and bright stripes of paint on his dark bare chest and cheeks was dancing to the rhythm of a thumping drum. Only, there wasn't a drummer. The music was provided by a stereo jam box leaning against the storefront. A crowd was gathered around him, further clogging the already busy sidewalk. At the end of the street a cloud of dust hovered over a gravel lot where a steady stream of cars and pickup trucks pulled in and out of parking spaces. After watching everything that was going on for a while, I started walking, hoping to find someplace where I could get a cold drink. I also needed to find somebody to ask where my grandfather lived.

I walked almost the entire length of the street, looking into shop windows. All the merchandise appeared to be Indian items—blankets, little totem poles, jewelry, moccasins, and feathered headdresses in all sizes. I finally found a small luncheonette and went inside. The air-conditioning was instantly refreshing. So I decided to splurge and spend some of my precious capital on a cold soft drink. I sat down at the counter on a high vinyl-topped stool and deposited the duffel bag at my feet.

"What'll it be?" a young man in a white jacket asked as he sponged the counter in front of me. He had long jet-black hair pulled neatly back into a ponytail, golden brown skin, and jet-black eyes that intrigued me because they were too dark to see any pupils. This was my first encounter with a real American Indian.

"I said what'll you have?" the young man repeated.

"Uh, a Coke," I replied, feeling embarrassed that I'd been caught staring.

He nodded and moved down the counter, collecting a tall old-fashioned-looking glass, dumping in a metal scoopful of little ice cubes, and then filling the glass from the spigot of a bright red machine with the familiar Coca-Cola logo.

"Seventy-five cents," he told me, setting the glass, a paper-covered plastic straw, and a small square paper napkin in front of me.

I quickly paid for my drink, and for the next few minutes I didn't think of anything except my ice-cold Coke. Once my thirst was quenched, though, I focused again on my purpose for being here.

"Excuse me," I said to regain the young man's attention as he passed in front of me.

"Something else?" he asked.

"Yes. I'm looking for someone. His name is John Ridge. Can you tell me where he lives?"

"John Ridge," the young man repeated as he prepared a hot fudge sundae that looked almost more wonderful than I could stand. "There are several families of Ridges around here. But, no. Sorry. I don't know a *John* Ridge. Sure you've got the right place?"

Chrissy's words instantly echoed in my mind. *"You don't know where he lives, do you?"*

"Yes," I insisted. "I know he lives in Cherokee or at least close to Cherokee."

"Yes, well, *close* could be anywhere," the young man informed me. "But if he lived on the Qualla Boundary, I'd have heard of him."

"Qualla Boundary?" I asked.

"Yes, that's what this whole area is called—the Qualla Boundary." The young man's smile was indulgent as if I'd said something that showed my ignorance. Before I could ask for a further explanation, though, an older man working behind the counter interrupted.

"You lookin' for John Ridge? Well, there's a Michael John Ridge over at the Catholic church. He died the day before yesterday. They're supposed to bury him this afternoon. Hope that's not the man you're looking for, but ..."

I didn't hear the rest of what he said. I suddenly felt as if I'd been slapped in the face. Grabbing my duffel bag, I left the luncheonette and began to walk woodenly back up the street lined with shops, in the direction from which I'd come. I couldn't remember if my grandfather's name had been *Michael* John, but that had been my father's name. It seemed like an uncomfortable coincidence. Could my grandfather have died before I'd even had a chance to meet him?

I stopped in a shop and asked directions to the Catholic church. It was only a couple of blocks away on a quiet street. A small sign posted on the door stated that the funeral for Michael John Ridge was scheduled for this afternoon at three o'clock. I went inside, but stopped in the vestibule and stood there, staring down the long aisle into the dimly lit sanctuary.

Suddenly, I was reminded of the funeral I'd just attended yesterday. I swallowed hard, fighting back the tears, but they still managed to spill out. The longer I stood there the more convinced I became that it was my grandfather in the coffin, but I had to be sure. I wasn't going back to Atlanta—back to four years of living with my aunt Mildred—without seeing my grandfather this once, even if he was dead. I might never know why he hadn't wanted me or why I'd been kept a secret from him, but at least I'd know what he looked like.

So I forced myself to walk down the long aisle to the altar. The only light was the rainbow splashes from the line of stained-glass panels on either side of the sanctuary and the one large stained-glass window behind the altar. The empty church was quiet. Very quiet. My footsteps sounded like drumbeats. Or was that my heart pounding?

The coffin was so high that I couldn't see anything but the blanket of flowers when I got up close. I tiptoed up to peer inside, and when I did, I sighed with relief.

The dead man was young. Michael John Ridge couldn't have been more than thirty.

"Can I help you, child?" someone asked from behind me.

I swung around, feeling embarrassed. I hadn't expected to be caught peeking into the coffin, and I realized how loud and out of place my expression of joy must have been. "I ... I ... was looking for someone," I stammered. "But it isn't him."

"Thanks be to God." The priest smiled at me. "Now, tell me who you're trying to find. I'm Father Paul, and I serve the people of this parish. Perhaps I can help you."

I didn't doubt that he knew the people of Cherokee. Slight of stature, dark-skinned, and with jet-black hair except where it was graying at the temples, Father Paul's Cherokee heritage was evident.

"I don't know," I told him. "I'm looking for John Ridge. He lives somewhere outside of Cherokee, and I thought maybe it was *just* outside—like in a suburb. But I don't think he ..."

"Yes, John Ridge," the priest interrupted. Father Paul's smile never seemed to diminish, so I wasn't sure if he repeated my grandfather's name to imply that he did know him or if he was simply acknowledging my request.

"A man at the luncheonette said that this man is Michael John Ridge," I added, to explain my presence.

"Yes," Father Paul agreed. "It is, but Ridge is a fairly common name here. Why are you looking for John Ridge?"

I almost lied, but this didn't seem the place to do that. Besides, I felt sure Father Paul would see right through any false reasons I might give. If he knew anything that might help me, I needed that information. "John Ridge is my grandfather," I admitted.

Now it was the priest's turn to look surprised. He leaned a little closer and peered at me intently, as though he were studying me. "The Lord doth work in mysterious ways," he announced finally with a broad smile that made me feel confused.

"Do you know him?" I asked. "The people I asked in town didn't seem to have heard of him."

"Oh, they know him well enough, but not by that name," Father Paul explained.

Of course. I wondered why I hadn't thought of it before. My grandfather had a nickname.

"So you do know where my grandfather lives? Is it close enough to walk?"

"Yes, I know where John Ridge lives," Father Paul told me. "But I'm afraid it's a considerable distance— probably a bit too far for you to walk. If you'll wait until later, when I'm free, I'll take you."

"I don't mind walking," I announced. "I'll find it, if you'll tell me how to get there." Just knowing that my goal was close suddenly made me feel terribly impatient.

"Well, all right—if you're sure. Come on. I'll show you the way to go." Father Paul led me back up the aisle and out the church door. "Walk along the highway there until you come to a road called Snowbird Mountain Trail," he said, pointing north. "Take Snowbird Mountain Trail until the road forks. Then bear to the right."

"And my grandfather's house is along that road?"

"No. John Ridge's house isn't on any road, but that's the one that comes the closest to it."

"But how will I know where to go from there?" I asked. "How will I find him?"

"Oh, don't worry. You'll find him," Father Paul promised. "If you walk along the right fork of Snowbird Mountain Trail, you'll find him. Or he'll find you."

The German shepherd barked, and I nearly lost my balance as I jerked in surprise at the noise. *I sure wish somebody would find me*, I thought. *I should've taken up Father Paul's offer of a ride.*

At that very moment, a man pushed through the bushes, boldly walked past the dog, and stood at the foot of the tree, looking up at me. He was clearly an Indian by his tawny skin, high cheekbones, and dark eyes, despite his being dressed in faded jeans and a plaid shirt with the long sleeves rolled up to his elbows. And he was obviously a very old Indian. His face was deeply lined with wrinkles, and the long hair sticking out below the cloth he'd wound around his head as a sort of turban was silver-white.

The Indian muttered something in a deep guttural voice that I didn't understand, though the German shepherd seemed to. It turned and darted away into the woods. Then the old man focused his full glowering attention on me.

Five

"Come down, and tell me why you're here," he said.

"I'm looking for John Ridge," I explained as I climbed down and brushed myself off. "Do you know him? Does he live near here?"

"Tell me why you want to see John Ridge." The little old man wasn't much taller than I was, but he stood there frowning down at me as though from a great height.

"I need to talk to Mr. Ridge," I said. Then I looked around because I heard a noise and saw the German shepherd returning, dragging my duffel bag. When the dog reached my feet, he stopped, looked up at me with angry brown eyes, and his black lips pulled back in a snarl. Then he let go of my bag and walked over to the Indian.

"I am Tsan," the old man announced very formally. "It's my name in the true language of my people, the

Tsa la ki, which you call the Cherokee. John Ridge is my English name, but I no longer answer to that name."

To say that I was shocked was the understatement of the year. This man—this old Indian—couldn't be my grandfather. If he was my grandfather, then I would have to be half Cherokee. But my father hadn't been an Indian—had he?

I remembered that my mother always said that I had my father's eyes, which were hazel but almost green. Did Indians ever have hazel-green eyes? This man's eyes were definitely not hazel. They were black polished stone boring into me, but I dredged up enough courage to meet his gaze and speak up.

"Didn't you have a son Michael?" I asked.

"Yes," Tsan answered, "but sadly he died long ago."

"Right," I agreed. "He's my dad. I mean he *was* my dad. I never knew him, because he died when I was just a baby, but my mom told me a lot about him." I paused. "She told me some really neat stories, like how he was a great baseball player and how ..." I saw Tsan's chiseled stone frown and shrugged. "But I guess you already know all that. Your son was my dad, so you're my grandfather," I added as if explaining this would help him understand his relationship to me.

"My son died when he was only a young boy," Tsan stated flatly. "So *you* cannot be my grandchild."

I noticed the old man had said *grandchild* not *granddaughter*. I wondered if this conversation would be going differently if I were a boy.

Tsan seemed to have read my thoughts. "Nothing would make any difference," he said. Then he cocked his head, studying me. "How did you get here?" he asked.

"I walked."

"From where?"

"From town, I ..."

"You're not from Cherokee."

"I didn't say I was. You didn't let me finish," I snapped. "I walked from town *after* I got off the bus from Atlanta."

"Who told you how to find me?" Tsan demanded.

"Father Paul. You know, the priest at the Catholic church? He offered to drive me up the mountain, but he was really busy, so I decided not to wait." I shrugged. "I had no idea what a long, hard walk it would be."

"You shouldn't have come," Tsan said, regarding me coldly. "Now go home, girl."

With that, he turned around and began walking away, signaling the conclusion of our conversation. It was clear I was dismissed.

I stood stiff and silent, stunned at Tsan's abruptness and shocked by everything that had just happened. Then something clicked inside me.

"I'm not leaving," I shouted.

Tsan stopped and turned around to look at me again.

"I'm *not* leaving," I repeated as if he hadn't heard me the first time. I picked up my duffel, still wet with dog saliva, and walked to where Tsan was standing.

"You must go," the old Indian declared angrily.

I straightened to my full height in order to meet Tsan's hard stare. "Why?" I asked.

"Because you don't belong here," the old Indian declared angrily.

"Are you telling me that I'm trespassing?"

"No man can own the earth any more than he can possess the air."

"Then I'm not leaving," I announced.

The German shepherd growled, as if to voice his own protest, and Tsan glared at me.

At last he muttered, "Do as you please, girl." Then he turned his back on me once again and walked toward the thick pine woods that lay directly ahead.

I felt triumphant for only a few seconds before I realized that I was being left on the side of the mountain with the afternoon rapidly slipping away. The sun was already a fat orange ball hanging just above the mountain's peak. If I stayed where I was, I'd soon find myself alone on the mountain at night. Where exactly was I going to stay?

The only logical answer was that I was going to stay with my grandfather, and I hurried after Tsan. After all, he had probably been as surprised by me as I had been by him. Older people were just more set in their ways and needed more time to adjust. If I followed him, he was sure to take me in, and then I'd have a chance to talk to him and show him the pictures of my mom and dad that I'd brought along. That should convince him I was telling the truth, and then maybe he'd explain to me what the big secret had been all these years.

Even more difficult to understand, though, was why Tsan had said that his son had died as a child. That didn't make any sense at all because I knew my dad was in his late twenties when he died. Maybe Tsan was just saying that because he didn't believe I was his granddaughter. Maybe *that* was why he was insisting I go away.

I was still thinking about what I would say to convince Tsan that he was my grandfather when we arrived at his house. It was more like a traditional log cabin than the Cherokee houses I'd seen in history books. Those log houses were plastered and white washed and had been built slightly dug into the ground, with short entrance tunnels, roofs of bark shingles, and a smoke hole opening at the center peak. Tsan's house sat on short stone columns. It had log walls chinked with red clay. The roof was covered with large bark shingles, but a thin curling finger of smoke rose from what appeared to be a red-clay-brick chimney at the back of the house. The windows on either side of the door were the single modern-looking fixtures. They were wood-framed glass panes, and the door was wooden, too, with a shiny brass knob.

A bench sat below the window to the left of the door under an extension of the roof that formed a small porch. The German shepherd immediately leapt to this bench and stretched out, laying his nose on one front paw. Without ever looking back at me, Tsan went inside and closed the door.

I started to walk slowly toward the house. The dog watched me approach. I got within ten feet of the porch steps before he sprang to his feet, growling and baring his teeth.

I jerked to a stop, not sure what to do. If he attacked, would Tsan come to my rescue?

I took one more step forward as a test. The German shepherd jumped off the bench and positioned himself so his back was toward the door and his sharp white teeth were aimed at me. I was now positive that he intended to keep me out of the house, and since Tsan neither opened the door nor called to the dog to back off, I was as good as locked out.

I stood where I was for a few minutes more, giving Tsan ample time to open the door. When he didn't, I backed up to the middle of the small clearing in front of the house. The dog immediately returned to the bench, but his large brown eyes never left my face as I stood staring at him and the house.

Tsan had obviously put something on to cook because the smoke that curled my way now carried a warm flavorful aroma. My mouth watered as I tried to identify the scent. I thought it might be bacon. The dog smelled the meat, too, because he lifted his nose, sniffed, and lapped a pink tongue across his hairy muzzle.

I decided I might as well have my own dinner and get settled. I was obviously on my own for the night. *At least I'm not entirely alone,* I thought miserably.

Even if I couldn't go inside, I felt safer just being close to Tsan's cabin, though it was hard to think of this grumpy old man as my grandfather. I wondered if my mother had gotten the same icy reception and that was why she had so totally shut him out of our lives. That didn't seem like enough of an explanation, though, and I found myself wondering again about "the secret," whatever had happened in the past to cause the family split.

I looked around the clearing and finally chose a spot next to two pines whose tall trunks grew close together. I spent some time scooping up pine needles and heaping them into a pile at the base of the trees to make a soft bed. After changing into jeans, I dug out one of the cheese sandwiches I'd brought with me, unwrapped it, and took a big bite. Chrissy had helped me pack, and she'd made me bring food, a flashlight, and a few other basics. I'd complained that I wasn't going to be camping out, but now I silently thanked Chrissy for insisting I be prepared. I swatted at a buzzing mosquito and wished I'd also packed insect repellent.

The sun was sinking fast. Only a faint orange glow penetrated the clearing now, and the woods surrounding the clearing were already full of dark shadows. The soft glow of a kerosene lamp shone in the windows of Tsan's small house. I sighed, wishing that that light was really as welcoming as it looked.

I suddenly felt very alone. I missed Chrissy. To my surprise, I even missed Josie and Becca. I took another bite of my rather stale cheese sandwich and thought longingly of eating hamburgers, fries, and milk shakes. I could almost taste them, and I wondered again if I'd done the right thing by coming here. I wondered, too, if Aunt Mildred and Uncle Frank had discovered my note and how they were taking my decision to run away. I hadn't told them where I was going, only not to worry, that I would be okay.

I hoped that Chrissy was keeping her promise not to tell anyone where I'd gone. She'd said that she could only hold out on her mother for just so long, and she'd have to tell her mother the truth once she discovered I'd borrowed the twenty dollars. And as soon as Mrs. Weber found out what Chrissy knew, she'd call my aunt. Of course, if my grandfather sent me away first thing in the morning, I might be back in Atlanta before anyone had a chance to come looking for me. I was determined not to give up and leave, though, without at least talking to my grandfather and showing him the photos I'd brought.

Gradually, the long shadows stretching out from the trees into the clearing grew wider until they merged. The pale gray half-light became night, and when I could no longer see clearly, the forest sounds seemed to become amplified. An owl hooted far away, and an answering hoot came from somewhere nearby. Besides the buzz of mosquitoes, there was a whole chorus of other insect voices, and a separate song was being sung by chirping tree frogs. I listened to all these sounds and wondered if there were bigger, silent creatures in the woods.

Suddenly, I heard the German shepherd jump down from the bench by Tsan's door. My breath caught in my throat, and I stopped chewing. The big dog's dark shadow slipped across the rectangular bright patch beneath Tsan's window and came toward me.

I dropped the sandwich into my lap and frantically rummaged through my duffel bag, searching for the flashlight I knew was in there—somewhere. My fingers churned through the rolls of tube socks and underwear as I heard the German shepherd coming closer.

At last my fingers closed on the cold metal cylinder. I pulled out the flashlight and panned the bright beam across the darkness in front of me. The German shepherd, only a few feet away, made a half-growl, half-whimpering sound.

"You're hungry, aren't you?" I asked softly. "I'll bet he doesn't feed you either." The dog pulled his black lips back in a snarl, but I felt less threatened now than I had before.

"Well, you certainly don't know how to beg," I told him. "I guess it's not your fault that you never learned any manners."

I pulled the remaining cheese sandwich out of my duffel bag, unwrapped it, and tossed it toward the dog. He snatched the sandwich out of the air and wolfed it down.

"You should eat more slowly and take time to enjoy it. That's all there is, you know." Whether or not he understood, the dog made no demands for more. With a final lick of the dusty place that had served as his plate, he ambled off into the woods.

Realizing what I'd just done, I felt foolish for giving away my last sandwich to a dog that was obviously more capable of providing for himself than I was. "Pretty stupid," I muttered.

A cool breeze had begun to blow. I put on my windbreaker and made a pillow out of my sweatshirt. Then I lay down on my pine-needle bed and tried to sleep. But sleep wouldn't come. I couldn't seem to stop my mind from thinking about all the *ifs*. If Tsan let me stay, but Aunt Mildred sent the police to find me ... If Tsan really made me leave ... If I went back to Aunt Mildred ...

I heard the patter of rain splattering on leaves before I felt the first drops as they filtered through the pine branches. Then I saw a bright flash of lightning and heard the thunder crash. Soon the air was full of rain. Whole curtains of water flowed across the clearing and blew into my face.

I pulled my knees up to my chest and huddled more tightly against the sturdy, rough tree trunk behind me. Waves of fear washed over me with the rain. I'd never been on a mountaintop in a storm, and I was amazed by how much more intense and frightening this storm was than any I could ever remember experiencing before. In fact, I used to enjoy snuggling in my big bed back home, feeling all the more safe and warm for the storm raging outdoors. There was no safe spot here. There wasn't even a dry spot.

As lightning flashed again, illuminating Tsan's house in an eerie blue light, I made a dash for the porch. The German shepherd was back at his post, though, and as soon as I got past the middle of the small clearing, he leapt to block my path.

I splashed to a stop in a big mud puddle and stood there hunched inside my windbreaker, clutching the neck opening closed under my chin. The German shepherd and I stared at each other through the rain. "Hey, I fed you," I pleaded.

The dog didn't growl, but he didn't move out of the way either. Then the lightning flashed again almost at the same instant that the thunder cracked, and a shiver rippled through me. That one was close!

I made a fast dash for the porch and sat down on the bench before I looked back at the German shepherd. The dog had followed me and was only a few feet away under the sheltering overhang of the roof. He tipped his big head up to look me in the eye, pulled his black lips back revealing sharp white teeth, and growled.

"I won't try to get into the house," I promised, "but I'm not going back out there. If you don't like it, you're going to have to drag me away."

The dog stared at me so hard I thought he was considering doing just that. Then suddenly he shook himself all over, showering me in water, and lay down at my feet.

Without saying anything else, I pulled my legs up on the bench and leaned back against the house. Then I remembered my duffel out by the pine-needle mound. Everything I had was probably getting soaked. The pictures might even be ruined.

I started to get up, but the German shepherd raised

his head and growled. The whole sky gleamed blue-white with yet another lightning flash, and the thunder crack vibrated through the wood cabin. The storm was still close. Very close. I pulled my legs up again and stayed where I was.

Six

I must have fallen asleep despite the storm's rumblings, because when I woke up, it was morning and the storm was gone. For a few seconds, I wasn't sure where I was or that I was really awake. The clearing was eerie and dreamlike as a thick, pearly mist floated in the air, making the pine tree trunks across the clearing look like strange ghostly figures.

I was thinking about how quiet it was when I realized that the dog was gone. I jumped off the porch and sprinted across the clearing to find my bag. There were deep puddles, but I splashed through them, not caring if my feet got wet again. The fog rolled out of the way in front of me until I stopped. Then the mist swirled back and swallowed me up as I stood still at the edge of the clearing, searching the woods for the twin pines.

It took me a few minutes to get oriented. I finally spotted the two tall dark trunks standing close together.

I found the pine-needle mound I'd made and my soggy sweatshirt lying on top of it. I knew I was in the right spot, but my duffel bag was gone.

Had the dog hauled it off somewhere? Maybe it had taken my bag to a favorite spot and was there right now, tearing through it, looking for something else to eat. I plowed into the mist-filled forest, wondering why I'd felt sorry for that miserable dog last night and fed it.

I'm not sure how long I had walked through the foggy woods before it occurred to me that I was lost. I turned around slowly, seeing dark tree trunks wrapped in mist that all looked the same. I wasn't even sure which trees I had passed only seconds earlier. How could I possibly retrace my steps? I leaned against a rough tree trunk, breathing hard. I was really, truly lost.

Was it only yesterday that I'd been afraid somebody would find me? Now, I was scared that nobody would even look for me. I doubted Tsan would. If he found me and my duffel bag gone, he'd probably just think I'd given up and left.

I took a deep breath, hunkered down to rest on my heels, and looked around me again. There might be a trail, I thought, but I would never see it in this pea-soup fog. Even without a trail, though, I should be able to find my way back if I marked my path and searched in each of the main compass headings for a given distance.

It was the German shepherd's sharp bark that brought me to my feet again. The sound seemed to be fairly close by, but I wasn't sure from which direction it came. I prayed for the dog to bark again.

And then he did. This time, I was sure enough to start moving in the direction I thought the sound had come from. But I hadn't gone very far before uncertainty made me hesitate. Had the sound really come from that direction? Or was it just an echo?

Bark again, please, I thought.

The silence seemed to go on forever. Then I heard the bark. It sounded more distant this time, as though the dog was going away from me rather than toward me. I ran in the direction of the dog's barks, trusting my senses and my instinct, and praying I wouldn't trip on a root or fallen branch buried in the fog.

CRACK! A loud noise sliced through the forest, and I jerked to a stop so fast that I slipped and fell, sprawling on the damp leaf-and-needle-covered forest floor. It had sounded like thunder, but the storm was over.

A gunshot, I thought. Maybe it was a hunter. I felt cold and sweaty, all at once. I lay very still, even though an uncomfortable dampness was soaking through my clothes, and the pungent odor of rotting leaves was unpleasantly strong so close to my nose. The dog's barks rose in a thunderous crescendo, and I could sense his fury. I wondered what made him so angry. Even when the German shepherd had threatened me, he had never sounded as vicious as he did now.

Then I realized that I could hear people too. I heard men's voices, but I could hear only snatches of words. The rumble of a car or a truck engine suddenly drowned out the men's voices, and when the engine noise faded, the men's voices were gone. The dog stopped growling and barking too. Instead, he howled. The sound was a soulful moan that seemed to go on forever.

I got up and cautiously eased through the fog and the forest toward the howling dog. Seconds later, I broke out of the forest and found myself in an area that had been logged clear. Land studded with stumps stretched bare to the crest of Snowbird Mountain on my left and as far below me as I could see on my right. Straight ahead of me, the German shepherd sat with his muzzle tipped skyward, howling, beside a gray lump on the ground. And everywhere wispy tendrils of mist twined like chimney smoke as they rose toward a fireball sun that was moon pale through the fog.

I knew even before I reached the dog that Tsan was the gray lump. The old man was facedown with his arms and legs bent at odd lifeless angles.

I was terrified as I dropped to my knees beside Tsan. I was afraid he was dead and afraid that the men I'd heard would return at any moment, or worse, that one of them might still be here—somewhere. I glanced around quickly, but I didn't see anyone. Then I rolled Tsan over onto his back.

There was a bright red stain growing on his shoulder and a puddle of blood on the ground. The dog nuzzled Tsan with his nose and lapped his tongue across the old man's cheek and ear.

Tsan's eyes flickered open a crack, and his jet-black vision focused on me. *"Hi hwi lo hi,"* he said in a voice that was little more than a whisper. "You must go."

I agreed with him. The best thing we could all do was get away from here. I quickly positioned myself on Tsan's uninjured side, draped his arm around my neck, wrapped my arm around his waist, and struggled to stand up. Tsan muttered something in his strange-sounding language that I assumed was a protest. When I finally had us both on our feet and felt in control, I looked down at the dog.

"Okay. You're going to have to show me the way home. And if you know any shortcuts, please take them."

The German shepherd immediately bounded down the clear-cut slope. I had no idea whether or not the dog was actually heading back to Tsan's cabin, but I could only trust that he was. Cutting across the cleared area was definitely easier than going through the woods. My fear that I'd run into the men who had shot Tsan intensified with each step, though. This had to be the way they'd gone. It was the only way they could have driven.

I moved as fast as I could, which wasn't very fast at all, and when I got too far behind, the big dog sprinted back and ran in a circle around me, barking. "I'm doing the best I can," I puffed.

"Ke?i hwi lo hi," Tsan grunted. I was surprised to hear him speak. He had been moving his feet so woodenly I wasn't sure he was completely conscious.

"What?" I asked.

"Downstream," Tsan mumbled, so softly that I wouldn't have understood at all if his mouth hadn't been next to my ear.

We were barely within the cover of the pine forest when the sounds of the bubbling stream were lost in the roar of a plane's engine starting up very close by. The German shepherd tensed and slowed, leading me with cautious steps deeper into the forest.

Through the screen of trees, I spotted a small white plane with red stripes across its wings and twin propellers—one on either side of its nose—a blur of spinning motion. A man with blond hair leaned out of the plane's side door and took a large black cloth bag from a tall, thin Indian man. He disappeared inside, but only seconds later he leaned out for a second bag. This bag wriggled so violently that there was no mistaking the movement. There was something alive in it, and the blond man had to grasp the sack with both hands as he hoisted it into the plane. He leaned out again, shouting something to the Indian that was lost to the engine roar and distance. Then the blond man closed the plane's door, and the Indian hurried back to an old Jeep parked off to one side of the clearing as the plane rolled away. The grassy meadow they were using as a runway was small, and the plane barely managed to lift off in time to clear the tall pines at the far end of the strip.

I didn't realize that I had stopped moving and was watching this scene unfold through the trees until the German shepherd nudged my leg. I obeyed this silent prodding and began moving forward again. Slowly, I followed the dog to the stream and stayed on his heels as we traced the water course down from the mountain's high ridge.

What were those men doing? What was in the black bags? Why did they shoot Tsan? My mind was racing with questions, but I didn't have time to think about the answers. Walking with Tsan and keeping my balance required too much concentration, and when he slumped heavily against me, the extra weight nearly knocked me down.

"Hang on," I ordered through clenched teeth as I struggled to straighten up and get a better grip by looping my fingers around the old man's belt. I felt desperate, realizing that if he did completely pass out, I wasn't going to be able to carry him the rest of the way home. "Hang on," I repeated.

It seemed a miracle when, a few minutes later, I saw Tsan's small house ahead of us through the trees. The mist was completely gone now, and the house looked bright and fresh against the dark green forest and azure-blue sky. The scene appeared unnaturally peaceful in light of the horrible events on the high mountain ridge.

"We're almost home," I told Tsan. He clearly needed a doctor, and without a phone I didn't know how I was going to get help in time.

The German shepherd hurried ahead of me across the clearing and up the steps to the cabin, but he didn't block my way this time as I helped Tsan inside.

It was difficult to see at first in the shadowy interior of the cabin, but there was no mistaking how sparsely furnished it was. There was only a rocking chair close to the fireplace, a table with two chairs in the middle of the room, and a narrow bed against the far wall with a large wooden trunk at its foot. My duffel bag sat on the table. I wondered when Tsan had gotten it and if he had looked through it and discovered the locket with my father's picture in it.

I walked Tsan across the room to the bed and helped him lie down. The German shepherd immediately sat down beside the bed and laid his muzzle on Tsan's hand. His whimper expressed the same helplessness I felt.

"What'll I do?" I asked aloud. It was a question for myself, but surprisingly Tsan opened his eyes just enough to peer at me from beneath heavy lids.

"Fetch a large handful of sassafras leaves," he said in a rattly whisper.

"Sassafras leaves?" I asked in surprise.

"Mmm," the old man confirmed with a grunt. "Sassafras stops bleeding."

"But, I ... I don't know ..." I stammered, "how to find a sassafras tree. I don't know what sassafras leaves look like."

Tsan's glowering frown was evident again now, and

this time when he spoke, his voice was stronger. "How old are you, girl?"

"Fourteen," I answered.

"How'd you get to be so old so stupid?" Tsan growled. "Get me paper and pencil." He lifted his uninjured arm and stabbed a finger into the air, pointing toward the large trunk at the foot of the bed. "In there."

I lifted the wooden lid and found the trunk full of books and stacks of paper with delicate beautiful pencil sketches of birds and animals and plants. I marveled at them and wondered if they were Tsan's work. I'd have to ask him about the drawings when he was well, but now, as quickly as I could, I searched for a blank sheet of paper. I found one and a stubby pencil that had obviously been sharpened with a knife. As I held the paper against a book, Tsan took the pencil and with a few quick motions scratched the image of a leaf. Rough as it was, the picture was lifelike and gracefully elegant. The leaf almost seemed to have floated down and landed on the page. I no longer had any doubt whose work I'd just viewed in the trunk.

"Sassafras," Tsan repeated, sagging deeper into the bed. "There's a tree not too far. Near the stream. Hurry," he added weakly.

Clutching the paper that was my guide to the only healing powers that were close at hand, I charged out of the cabin and ran in search of a sassafras tree.

Seven

With Tsan's sketch to help me, I found the sassafras tree. I wasn't sure how many leaves were needed so I took off my windbreaker, tied the sleeves together to make a sort of bag, and stuffed it full of leaves. Then I ran back to the cabin with my prize.

"You must pull open the shirt so the compress can be placed directly on the wound," Tsan instructed me, as I knelt beside his bed. My fingers fumbled with the buttons. "Tear it," he told me.

I grabbed the flannel cloth on either side of the buttons and yanked. The shirt opened with a sharp rip, and my breath caught in my throat as I stared down at the bullet wound.

"Lucky. Bullet went clear through," Tsan said in short gaspy phrases. "But got to stop bleeding. Chew the leaves and press the compress on both sides of my shoulder. Press where there is the most blood."

"What?" I gulped, swallowing hard.

"Chew. Make pulp," Tsan said gruffly. *"No: kwa!"*

Obeying his command, I stuffed one of the sassafras leaves into my mouth and began to chew. It tasted bitter and green, and as some of the liquid slipped down my throat I gagged, spitting out the pulp.

"Don't swallow," Tsan instructed.

He probably waited to tell me that on purpose, I thought angrily. But Tsan's closed eyes, pale face, and tightly drawn expression were enough to make me chew more leaves—fast. Finally, there was enough pulp to cover the wound. As I pressed the mushy compress against his skin a groan as soft as air escaping from a squeezed bag slipped from Tsan's dry lips.

I was startled by the coolness of the old man's skin. Shock, I thought, remembering what I'd learned in first aid. I used books to prop up Tsan's feet and spread my sweater and sweatshirts over his thin bare chest. There was already a scar on his chest. It looked like a ragged lighting bolt cutting through the wiry silver hair.

"Oak bark," Tsan whispered, as I leaned over him, adjusting my makeshift blanket. "Boil it in water. Cover it, and let it sit for ten minutes. Then give me the tea." He opened his eyes just a slit and said, "You know what an oak tree is?"

"Yes, I can find an oak tree," I snapped, searching my duffel bag for the pocketknife Chrissy had insisted I bring. I knew what oak leaves looked like, though it took a while to find an oak tree among the pine forest. I pried off chunks of the tough bark and returned to the cabin, figuring the hardest part of my job was over.

But making the tea turned out to be a lot more difficult than preparing the compress. First, I had to find a pot for the water. Next, I had to get some water from the well behind the house, but even though I pumped and pumped until my arms ached, not a drop of water dripped out of the spout.

Then I spotted a bucket of water nearby and recalled that strange expression: prime the pump. I carefully poured the bucket of water into the open top of the pump and began to work the handle again. This time, my efforts were rewarded almost instantly. Water gushed out, filling my pot to overflowing. I dumped out the first potful just to be sure what I collected was really clean and refilled the priming bucket before I quit pumping. I was trying desperately not to do anything that would give Tsan a fresh opportunity to find fault.

Boiling the water proved to be the biggest challenge of all. I couldn't figure out how to turn on the black iron stove until it dawned on me that you had to build a fire in it. Somehow I doubted that even the home economics class I was supposed to take next year would prepare me for this situation.

I went outside again and discovered a neat stack of firewood under a lean-to at the side of the house. There was also a small storehouse elevated on posts, a fenced pen with three goats and one kid, a coop with about a dozen chickens, and a small garden where beans and squash plants were growing around the prop roots of tall corn stalks. I was suddenly very impressed with the old man. Tsan had built more than just a cabin on the high ridge of Snowbird Mountain. He'd built a whole, self-sufficient little world. The ability to be independent was something I'd come to appreciate in the past week.

I carried my armful of small split sticks to the fireplace and carefully stacked them into a log cabin pattern the way we always did at Girl Scout camp. Then I placed a handful of dry pine needles on the sticks and lit this paper-dry clump with the matches I'd packed wrapped in plastic in my duffel.

Flames leapt up instantly, and feeling proud, I went back outside for an armload of logs. The kindling was burning well when I returned, so one by one I added the logs. The fire began to crackle and pop. Flames shot up the chimney. I poked the dry, burning wood with the iron shovel, and the heat blasted my face. My little fire had quickly become a roaring blaze. I thought I could feel Tsan's jet-black eyes staring at me disapprovingly, but when I glanced over my shoulder at him he still had his eyes closed—apparently asleep.

Keep calm, I thought. I'd used too much kindling and then added the firewood too quickly. The fire singed the hair on my arms as I used the shovel to knock a couple of logs to one side. They rolled together, sending up a swarm of sparks.

Some of the sparks shot out and landed on the ancient hearth rug. I hurried to stamp them out before the rug caught on fire. As I stamped I thought I felt Tsan watching me again, but when I turned around and looked, he was still lying with his eyes shut.

After nearly an hour, the fire finally died back to the mound of glowing red coals I'd planned to create in the first place. Relieved, I brought the pot of water to the fireplace and realized that I had no way to set it over the flames. Fresh frustration made me angry, angry at the tea I was supposed to make, angry at Tsan for telling me to make it without telling me how to do it. Most of all, I was angry at myself.

Tsan was right. I was stupid.

I wasn't stupid in Atlanta, but that was because I'd learned the things you needed to know to function successfully in a city—like how to operate a microwave oven, how to set a VCR to record up to fourteen separate programs, and what bus and train to take to go shopping at Lenox Square Mall.

Okay, I vowed. *I wasn't going to be stupid here anymore.* I was going to learn how to do the things you needed to know to function on Snowbird Mountain. Number one—I was going to learn how to boil water on a wood-burning stove.

Twenty minutes later, I ladled golden brown tea into a chipped mug and carried the steaming brew to Tsan. He was sweating and restless. He'd knocked off the clothes covering him, and the compress had slipped off the wound. There was a small puddle of fresh blood on his chest. As I gently pressed the compress back over the wound, I noticed his skin felt hot and feverish.

"Drink this, Tsan," I urged, lifting his head while I held the cup to his lips.

"Ta ka no hi:li. U wo ha? li. Ti:ye:? stih ski," he told me with such great concern in his voice that I wished I understood.

"It's all right," I assured him. "Drink some of your tea. It's oak bark tea, just like you ordered."

He took several long sips as I tipped the cup, and I watched the bump of his Adam's apple roll up and down in his thin neck as he swallowed. When he was lying down again, I checked the sassafras compress one more time. Then I got another pot full of water from the well and a cloth to sponge his feverish skin.

As I bathed Tsan, the German shepherd, who had been

lying stretched out on the floor at the head of Tsan's bed, came over and sat down beside me. The big dog cocked his head to one side and regarded the old man with sad brown eyes.

"I don't want to lose him either," I said, reaching out to pat the dog's head. The German shepherd snarled, curling his black lips back to expose his sharp white teeth.

"Okay! Okay!" I jerked my hand back. "I understand. You're tolerating my presence because I'm useful. Well, let me tell you something, dog. You aren't exactly my favorite creature either."

Maybe the dog was growling because he was hungry. I looked around for dog food but there was none around. Since he returned to his position at the head of Tsan's bed, I decided to wait until Tsan got up to ask him if I should feed the dog. Tsan seemed to be resting comfortably, so I decided to take a closer look at the pictures in the trunk. I took them out and sat down cross-legged on the floor where the sun was now streaming through the window. One by one I looked at the pictures and then spread my favorites out on the floor in front of me.

The creatures Tsan had drawn appeared so alive that the animals and birds and wildflowers nearly burst from the pages. Those pictures could have been done only by a man who really loved the things he was drawing. I looked at Tsan's wrinkled face—looking angry at the world even as he slept—and wondered at the contradiction that seemed to exist between the man who had done these sketches and the one who was here with me.

The pictures gave me another reason for wanting to know Tsan. I had a box full of my own sketches in my closet back in Atlanta. My mother had always told me my artistic ability was a special gift. Maybe my grandfather was the person my gift had come from.

The German shepherd's sudden growl alerted all my senses as if it were an alarm clock's ring. I don't know why I looked straight at the window, but I did. My eyes locked on those of a young Indian man with a long thin face, a rather large nose, a small tight line for a mouth, and a thick shock of black hair. A shiver rippled through me as I recognized him. Even though I'd only seen him from a distance, I knew this was the Indian who had handed the black bag to the man in the plane.

Eight

"The door!" I shouted as the face disappeared from the window. I grabbed the rocker and shoved its back under the knob. Then I ran to the kitchen area and grabbed the only weapon I could find quickly—Chrissy's pocket-knife. I stood in the middle of the cabin with the knife raised, looking from the windows to the door and back to the windows—listening, watching.

The only sounds were the fire crackling and the German shepherd's growling from beside Tsan's bed. The only thing visible through the windows was the woods. Fear was making me tremble, and I backed up until I had the cabin wall to lean on.

I'd rather know where he is, I thought. What did he want?

Witnesses. Whatever this man and the others had been doing on Snowbird Mountain was probably illegal. They'd shot Tsan because they didn't want any witnesses. This man had gone—or been sent—back to take care of the body. Only there hadn't been a body, so he'd come looking. And now he knew there was another witness.

Only I didn't see what happened. But, of course, this man doesn't know that. He may think I was watching from the woods. Or he may think that Tsan has told me what happened.

If they were willing to shoot Tsan, they're willing to kill anyone that could tell the police about them.

I realized that the dog had stopped growling. Did that mean that the man had gone away? Why would he? Why didn't he just break in and shoot us if he had a gun?

All I had was Chrissy's knife, but I wouldn't have known how to use a gun if I'd had one. I looked at the pocketknife in my hand. I wasn't sure that I'd be able to stab anyone. Well, maybe, if I had to.

I licked my dry lips. I wished again that I knew where the man was.

Maybe he's waiting for it to get dark. If that was the case, then we might have time to escape. I'd gotten lost so quickly in the woods this morning that I didn't think we'd have to go very far from the cabin to hide. I thought I might be able to slip out somehow when it first started to get dark. Twilight was the hardest time to see the difference between shadows and real objects.

But what about Tsan? I thought. I looked at him asleep on his bed. How could I escape with him too?

I was frightened, knowing that someone was trying to kill us. The need to survive is a strong tonic, though, and I was able to think clearly about our predicament. As the hours passed, I worked on a plan. Periodically, I gave Tsan more of the oak bark tea, hoping this would break the fever. Remembering that the house was set up on short stone columns, I used a bigger kitchen knife and the fireplace shovel to pry loose boards from the kitchen floor. The hole wasn't quite big enough for me to squeeze through at first, so I chipped the wood away to enlarge the hole. By late afternoon, it was finally big enough for me to slip down through the floor.

As I let myself down feetfirst I tried not to think about the slithery snakes that might be lurking in the cool shadows under the house. I dropped to the ground and crawled across the bare, stony soil until I could look out between the porch steps.

I didn't see the young Indian man at first. He was stretched out on my pine-needle mound with his back to the twin pines and a shotgun across his lap. He looked as if he were asleep. I was tempted to make a run for it right then and go for help, but I remembered how far away help was. And as I stared at the shotgun I thought about how helpless Tsan was.

Something furry rubbing against my leg made me flinch. The dog had followed me out of the cabin and was lying on his belly directly beside me.

"Go back," I ordered in a harsh whisper. "You can't help me this time."

Suddenly, too quickly for me to grab him, the dog sprang forward. I watched—stunned—as it became a gray-brown blur, tearing across the clearing in front of the cabin.

That stupid dog, I thought desperately. *He'll spoil everything!*

Just as I'd feared, the Indian jumped to his feet, cocking the gun in his hands as he rose. First, he swung the shotgun in a wide arc in front of him. Startled from sleep, he obviously wasn't sure what was going on either. Any second, I expected to see him charge up the porch steps and blast his way into the cabin. Then there was a loud unmelodious chorus of squawks, and he took off in the direction of the chicken coop.

Yes! I couldn't believe my good fortune. That dog had created the perfect distraction. Now was my chance to try to get Tsan out of the cabin and escape. Without wasting another second, I crawled back to the hole and pulled myself up into the cabin. Tsan was propped up on his uninjured arm.

"What's happening?" he asked.

"Trouble!" I hurried to pull the rocker out of the way and open the door.

"What's happening?" Tsan repeated.

"One of the men that shot you is here, and he's got a gun." I sat down beside Tsan on the bed, put his uninjured arm around my shoulders, slipped my arm around his waist, and stood up, pulling him with me. "We've got to get into the woods and hide."

"Ata: lo: nu heh ski," Tsan growled. "Traitor."

We made it through the door and down the steps, but the going was a lot slower than I'd hoped. I prayed that it wasn't *too* slow.

"This isn't your problem," Tsan grumbled. "Leave me and get out of here."

"It's my problem now." I was puffing. "He saw me through the window." I struggled to move faster, dragging the old man with me. Tsan was making an effort to match his strides to mine, but he wasn't very successful. We crossed the clearing in a hobbling half-walking, half-running gait like contestants in some weird race.

"It doesn't matter," Tsan insisted. "You're quick. Run! You can get away."

"I'm not going without you." I was pushing for even more speed now that we were nearing the cover of the pine forest.

"Why?" he growled in my ear. "Why don't you just go?"

A shotgun blast punctuated our rush into the shadowy refuge of the dense woods, and I quickly glanced over my shoulder. I didn't see the Indian.

"Because you need me," I answered, and then I added, looking the old man in the eye. "Because I don't have anyplace else to go."

"Your mother has a sister," Tsan stated.

"Not an acceptable option," I replied. "Hey, I didn't mention her. If you know about her, you must have known about me. Did you?"

He didn't answer my question because just then another shotgun blast split the relative quiet on Snowbird Mountain. After that, Tsan and I concentrated all our attention and effort into putting distance between ourselves and the cabin. Once we were deep in the forest, the question became which way to go.

"There," Tsan hissed in my ear as we hobbled into the cover of the trees.

"What?" I asked, trying to decide which way he meant.

"Up," he instructed. "Up the ridge."

I looked in the direction he was indicating. Rugged gray boulders protruded from the leaf litter, and the ground inclined sharply. It was clearly the hardest way to go.

"Absolutely not," I said. "We're going down along

the stream until we find another cabin or reach the highway.

"No." Tsan stopped so suddenly that I was taken by surprise. I only barely managed to keep my balance.

"C'mon," I said. "There isn't time to argue. We've got to find help." I tried to start moving again, but Tsan continued to resist me. This time I tried to pull away from him, but he hung onto me with a bony grip that was surprisingly strong.

"This is the only way," he persisted.

"I never met anyone so stubborn," I complained, but I started moving in the direction he wanted to go anyway.

I regretted my decision immediately. The going was even harder than I'd anticipated, and it wasn't long before we were both stumbling and panting.

"We've ... we've ... got to go ... back down," I managed between breaths.

"No," Tsan insisted. "Up!"

I gave in again only because the top of the ridge seemed closer than a retreat toward the stream. But I kept looking back over my shoulder for the young Indian. We were sitting ducks if he spotted us—two easy targets on a rock wall. Amazingly, he didn't appear, and we eventually made it to the top of the ridge.

"Now what?" I asked, panting, checking behind us yet one more time.

"Down," Tsan informed me.

A sheer rock cliff dropped twenty feet to a rock outcrop directly below us, and beyond that the mountainside remained steep as it descended into a thick forest of mixed pines and hardwoods.

"You've got to be kidding," I said.

"We must hurry," Tsan retorted.

"How? I didn't bring any rock-climbing gear—not even a rope. No. This is it. Now we've really got to turn around and go back."

"Only *Ani: yo: wa ne: ka*—whites—are so blind," Tsan fumed. "If you were even part *Ayv:wi yá hi*—brown person—as you claim, you'd go down that ledge quickly."

"That's a ledge?" I stared at the skinny lip of rock, protruding from the sheer cliff.

"We'll have to walk separately," Tsan said.

"B-but—"

"Don't worry. I'll manage it," Tsan told me, taking his arm from around my shoulders.

"Yeah. Well, that's good to know," I snapped.

"*No: kwa!*—now—go!" he commanded, prodding me with his uninjured hand.

"Don't push," I protested, but I cautiously put one foot in front of the other.

My stomach was doing somersaults. I tried not to look down, but when my foot kicked some loose gravel over the edge, I looked.

It was a long, *long* way down the gray rock wall. I thought, *If I slip and fall, it's going to be a long, long fall.* My stomach did cartwheels as I thought about landing on the rocks below.

"Keep going." Tsan's bony finger poked between my shoulder blades.

"Stop pushing me," I protested again, but I forced myself to start inching forward again.

I have no idea how long it actually took me to reach the jutting outcrop of rock, but if I had to guess, I'd say a hundred years—at least. When I'd made it at last, I looked back up the cliff's rock face, and thought, *Don't tell me I'm going to have to climb back up to go back to the cabin.*

"There's another way back," Tsan said, as though he'd read my mind. "This way is just the shortest."

"You mean I could have come down from the ridge some other way?" I demanded. "Why didn't you tell me?"

Tsan ignored my question as he leaned heavily—weakly—against the rocks. I hurried to slip my arm around his waist before he collapsed. With what I suspected was rather grudging gratitude for my assistance, the old man put his arm back around my neck and leaned on me.

"How far is it to another cabin?" I asked. "We need to get to a telephone so we can call the police."

"No," Tsan told me.

"No what? No cabin or no telephone?"

"No help," Tsan stated. "It wouldn't do any good to call police. There are no charges I can bring. These men were stealing, but they'll say they weren't. I have no proof."

"Stealing? Stealing what?"

"Birds—eagles this time. I have seen them come before, taking falcons and hawks. I've grieved that these creatures of the *Thu: thi*—the Snowbirds—should be taken away from their home. I've felt the anger of the *Nv: ne hi*—sacred people of the mountain—grow each time the white men have come and stolen. But I did nothing, telling myself each time that surely this is the last time. If I say nothing, these men will go away and all will be peaceful."

"Only they came back again, and this time they caught you watching them," I finished for him.

"No," Tsan stormed. "This time, when I saw how cruelly these men acted, taking both eagle parents, so that the little ones would die, too, the *Nv: ne hi* yelled to the warrior in me, saying, "*U hóh saa*—Be strong!"

"I slipped around behind the men, to steal away the one eagle parent tied up inside a bag, while they were busy capturing the other eagle parent. The white men would not have heard me. Their ears do not hear the forest voices. But that traitor who takes money from the white men for his betrayal—he heard."

A few pebbles clattering down the sheer rock face of the cliff made us freeze. I knew we were both thinking of the traitor Indian. I might have stood where I was, staring up the cliff in rigid terror until I was spotted, if Tsan hadn't forced me into motion again.

Silently, and with a burst of strength, the old man tugged me over to the cliff. We flattened ourselves against the rock, and Tsan began to inch along the wall, intent on reaching some destination. I followed, afraid to be left behind.

More pebbles rained down, bouncing when they hit the rocky outcrop. There was definitely someone up above us, and the odds were pretty much in favor of it being the young Indian with the shotgun.

Tsan tapped my arm to get my attention and motioned for me to follow. I watched as he scooted around a boulder that filled up the narrow rock outcrop and disappeared. When I followed him around the boulder, I discovered a narrow opening in the cliff face. It was a cave, but I couldn't see past the opening.

My mind rebelled at the thought of going into the cave. It looked spooky and forbidding. It probably had bats, or bears.

No, I definitely don't want to go in there, I thought.

Then I heard a sound. I wasn't sure, but I thought it

was someone—probably the traitor Indian—coming down the ledge.

I took a deep breath, ducked to squeeze through the low, narrow opening, and plunged into the dark cave.

Nine

I didn't know where Tsan was. I couldn't see him. The darkness was blacker than any night I'd ever known. I couldn't even see my own hands in front of me. I reached out, feeling for Tsan, but I didn't touch him. All I found was cold, slimy rock. I was afraid to say anything for fear the sound would carry and give our hiding place away. But I had the eerie sensation that I was on the brink of falling. I was afraid to move, so I sat down where I was, just far enough inside the cave that I couldn't be seen by anyone.

What would I do if I heard the Indian coming closer? I sat still and listened. Tsan had belittled the white man's sense of hearing, and I wondered if there was too much white blood in me to let my ears adequately warn me of approaching danger.

An instant later, I had my answer. Without any warning sound that I could detect, a dark shape suddenly blocked most of the bright slit of the cave entrance. I shrieked and was immediately rebuked by a warning hiss from Tsan behind me.

The thing coming into the cave let out a half whine, half snarl. "It's only the dog," I announced, greatly relieved.

"Shhh," Tsan whispered. "It wasn't Nv?ya on the cliff. He came around through the forest."

How did Tsan know that? I wondered, but I felt safer knowing that Tsan was close and listening with full-blooded Indian ears that could hear such things. Then the German shepherd ran his furry muzzle along my leg, sniffing me, making himself sure of me. I scratched behind his ears, thinking, *So, dog, you have a name. Nv?ya.*

We stayed still in the dark a long time. Then finally, Tsan reported: "The traitor is gone."

"Good. Then let's get out of here." I started to move toward the cave entrance, but Tsan's bony hand closed over my arm. I wondered if full-blooded Indians could also see better in the dark.

"No. Sit still," he told me. "That traitor could be watching. He's more clever and determined than I thought. We must wait to leave until the night begins to swallow up the day. But then I agree that we must go down the mountain. Soquah and his family live down this side of the Snowbird."

"Do they have a phone? I know what you said before, but we have to call the police. Maybe we can't prove that these men have been poaching, but Tsan, they tried to kill you. This man is trying to kill *us.*"

"There is danger, *to hi yu*—true." Tsan's voice sounded sad. "I will call the Agency."

I wasn't sure what the Agency was, but it sounded

awfully legal. I felt relieved, but I didn't want to wait. I hated being inside this cave. I was cold, I was thirsty, and I was hungry. But I sat still and didn't say anything. Tsan was right, it was safer to stay hidden inside the cave until twilight.

"I am very tired," Tsan said. "Now that Nv?ya's here, we can trust him to warn us if the traitor comes again. I'm going to get some sleep. It will be a long, difficult walk down the mountain tonight. You should try to rest, too, girl."

"Kate," I corrected him.

"What?" It was a grumpy grunt.

"My name isn't *girl*," I told him. "It's Kate. It's Kathleen really, but everybody I know calls me Kate."

"Mmmm, should be *ta wih ska la.*"

"What's that mean?" I demanded.

"*Ta wih ska la* means flint. You're like flint. When struck you don't break, you give sparks."

I wasn't sure whether or not I was being insulted, but I didn't think so. Tsan's tone had been surprisingly kind. In fact, I decided being called *ta wih ska la* was a compliment—almost.

I didn't think that I'd be able to sleep, but I did. And I dreamed about eaglets, shrieking for their parents. But no matter how loudly they cried, no eagle swooped down, bringing food to their treetop nest. I awoke uttering a stiffled cry of my own, with Tsan gently jostling my shoulder.

"What is it?" he asked. I told him about my dream. "It's the eaglets' *a nih ski:na*—spirits," he told me. "The Raven Mockers—the evil spirits—are sucking away their life breath, and the little ones are trying desperately to survive. The eagle is a bird of great courage. It's an omen that these little ones have spoken to you."

"But what kind of omen?" I asked. I was still feeling shaken by my nightmare. Waking up hungry and cold in this slimy darkness was making me feel more disturbed instead of reassured.

"I'm not an *ata: wé hi*—a wizard—so I could not say. Perhaps it is only a warning for us to be all the more alert tonight."

That seemed like good advice to me.

"I'm feeling stronger for my rest," Tsan added. "Too bad I don't have my hunting pouch of *se:lu*—corn—so we might eat a handful of the kernels."

Dried corn? I'd been thinking longingly of pizza—pepperoni, sausage, black olive, and extra cheese. My mouth watered at the mere possibility, but I doubted that Domino's would deliver to Tsan's cabin even if I could get to a phone. Then I remembered that I hadn't fed Nv?ya and I felt bad. "I didn't feed Nv?ya before because I couldn't find the dog food."

"Nv?ya takes care of himself," Tsan said. "He hunts his own food." He paused, then added, "We'll find water along the way, and our empty stomachs will make the food that Anisee, Soquah's wife, prepares for us taste all the better."

The promise of food and safety made me eager to be off, but Tsan insisted on going out first. He crawled over me and then disappeared through the rock crack. Nv?ya bumped my arm with his head after Tsan left and rubbed his muzzle against my hand.

"Are you trying to make friends?" I asked. When a wet nose pushed under my palm, I cupped my fingers around it.

After a wait so long that I had begun to worry, a sharp

hiss from the cave entrance summoned Nv?ya and me. A cool breeze brushed my face as I emerged, and the pine-scented evening wind was as sweet as perfume.

The sunset was even more spectacular than the one I'd witnessed the night before. The fireball sun was already gone, and the remaining daylight trailing after it was painting the sky. The colors ranged from a brilliant, deep rose closest to the mountaintop, through a soft mauve, a deeper purple, and then to a charcoal gray. The tall trees thrust black spikes into the colorful tapestry.

I thought the world looked too peaceful to be dangerous. The forest was silent except for the wind and the night's first owl *who-whooing* from somewhere deep within the woods.

"Stay close," Tsan ordered. I nodded. It was an unnecessary order.

Tsan was walking without my assistance now, and he led the way. I followed, and Nv?ya stayed close too. The German shepherd made me nervous by frequently stopping and staring into the shadows with his ears perked up. Sometimes he lifted his pointed nose as if sniffing something. I wondered what the dog sensed that I didn't. Then a fat raccoon loped across our path.

"How much farther?" I asked after we'd walked for some time. Tsan's only answer was a shushing noise that he cast over his shoulder at me. We were well below the cliff now. I felt sure we were safely undercover, and it was rapidly getting dark. Mist was forming, too, filling in the spaces between the trees with eerie, filmy shapes.

"Look, I only want to know ..." I began. Tsan hissed at me at the same instant that Nv?ya growled. I stopped talking and stopped moving. All my senses keyed to penetrating the darkness in the direction Nv?ya was facing. The twilight, I suddenly realized, was as good a cover for the young Indian as it was for us.

Tsan stepped into the long shadow of a tall pine just as the shotgun blast ripped through the evening quiet. Nv?ya growled, and Tsan's hand snagged my arm, pulling me next to him.

"Stay here," he told me. Then he was gone.

A second shotgun blast wrenched through the shadows. I huddled against the rough tree trunk, wishing I could press myself inside it. I heard Nv?ya barking and the sounds of a struggle.

Tsan couldn't be fighting with the young man. He wasn't strong enough to win. What could he be thinking of?

Nv?ya's sharp cry of pain was unmistakable. Then the forest was quiet again. My ears ached from listening for a sound—any sound—that would tell me what was happening. But I couldn't hear anything except my heart pounding and the night wind making the pine boughs bump into each other. I pinched my lower lip between my teeth and peered wide-eyed into the foggy dark forest. Was Tsan dead? Was Nv?ya?

The young Indian leapt toward me dragging the mist with him. His raised arm swung down, thrusting a knife at me. I shrieked and jerked sideways. The knife missed me—barely—and stuck in the tree's trunk.

The Indian needed a few seconds to pull the knife free. I launched myself into the dark, mist-filled forest, running. I didn't know where I was going. I didn't care as long as it was away. I could taste blood. I must have bitten my lip when the young Indian jumped me.

I couldn't look back to see if I was being followed. I needed to keep my eyes focused ahead, trying to avoid obstacles that were hard to see in this almost night. I swerved around a tree, stumbled, but stayed on my feet this time. I was making too much noise. I'd be easy to track. I thought I should stop and hide. The mist was getting so dense, I might be able to hide if I just sat down and was still. Hiding definitely seemed like a good idea, but I was too afraid to stop.

So I ran, wondering if I was going toward Soquah's cabin or away from it. I was lost again, but I doubted my pursuer was. Then I saw the glimmer of a light ahead of me in the woods. The glowing ball floated strangely in the thick fog and I felt flooded with relief as I ran toward it. But as quickly as it had appeared, the light disappeared.

I couldn't help the cry of dismay that slipped through my lips. I struggled to run faster before the person went away. I heard a snap like a twig breaking in the darkness very close behind me. I looked. It was the Indian.

"Help!" I shouted. Then I broke out of the trees. I was back in the clearing in front of Tsan's cabin. I'd run in a circle. With the moon rising above the high crest of Snowbird Mountain, I could see the cabin door standing open. Tsan's chickens were scattered across the clearing in front of the house, pecking at the dirt. I was about to run into the cabin and shut the door when a steely arm wrapped around my neck from behind.

"Now I've got you." The Indian's voice was loud in my ear. I struggled to pull free, clawing at the arm that held me. The Indian quickly put an end to my efforts by wrapping his free arm around me, too, pinning me firmly against himself.

"No, you don't!" shouted an authoritative voice from behind the Indian. "Let her go."

The arms holding me miraculously opened, and I staggered away a few steps. When I turned around, I saw Nv?ya and Tsan emerge from the forest. Tsan was carrying the young Indian's shotgun. He jerked the gun up, but it wasn't needed. The traitor was already staring down the barrel of a rifle. We'd all been rescued by Father Paul.

Ten

"Over here," Father Paul called, and two men carrying flashlights and rifles came around from the other side of the cabin. Both men were dressed in uniforms. I understood as Father Paul and Tsan talked to them that they were with what Tsan had called the Agency, the Bureau of Indian Affairs for the Qualla Boundary, which was the Cherokee Indian Reservation in North Carolina.

The young man was handcuffed and led away between the two men to a Jeep. And when they had gone, the three of us—plus Nv?ya—went into the cabin. Tsan quickly lit the lamp on the table. A few glowing coals remained from the fire I had built. It was enough for Father Paul to prod into life with a handful of dry pine needles, a few pieces of kindling, and then a fresh dry log.

"I wanted to be sure you two were getting along all right," Father Paul explained. Tsan was once again settled in bed, and Father Paul was dressing his shoulder with antibiotic ointment and a gauze bandage he had taken from a first aid kit in his backpack.

"You can imagine my surprise when I found the cabin open and the chickens out of their coop," Father Paul told us. "Not like you, Tsan." The old man shook his head in agreement.

"It's for moments such as these that my good parishioners have equipped my Jeep with a radio. I got your rifle, Tsan. Then I called the patrol."

"You have been a good friend to us," Tsan announced. "You must stay for dinner."

"I'll do better than that. I'll cook it." Father Paul's smile was contagious. "And I'll stay the night. Breathing this crisp clean mountain air tonight will be good for me—just what I need." The truth, of course, was that he was just what we needed.

While Tsan rested, I helped Father Paul prepare what he called "good Indian food." It was a sort of corn meal porridge with thin strips of dried meat simmered in it. I didn't know what kind of meat it was, and I wasn't sure about the strange appearance of this food. The aroma of the porridge bubbling in the pot made my mouth water, though, and when a helping was scooped into a wooden bowl for me, I quickly sampled it.

"Like it, Kate?" Father Paul asked.

"It's great!" I said. Then I stopped shoveling the porridge into my mouth and stared at Father Paul. I remembered that I'd carefully avoided telling him my name. Alarm bells went off in my mind with the realization that he knew who I was. Had he already called Aunt Mildred? Were the Agency police coming back for me in the morning? Perhaps the real reason Father Paul was staying was to make sure I didn't run away again.

Father Paul appeared unaware of my concern as he took a bowl of food to Tsan and then gave his full attention to his own meal. I finished my food in silence. Father Paul washed the few dishes in an enamel pan full of water he'd heated on the stove, and I dried. When we finished, the priest took the lamp and started for the door.

"Come help me, Kate," he called. "We won't be able to pen up the chickens tonight, but at least we can feed them. And the goats need tending too." I followed, feeling that it was my duty to help Tsan if only this one last time. Nv?ya chose to remain in his favorite place at the head of Tsan's bed.

"Don't worry about your grandfather," Father Paul told me, once we were alone, putting sweet-smelling hay into troughs for the goats. "He's strong, but he will have to rest for a few days. Tomorrow you'll need to herd the goats out to the meadow below the road," he told me. "This hay should be saved for the winter. Nv?ya will help you."

"Will I be here tomorrow?" I blurted.

"Why wouldn't you?" Father Paul sounded genuinely shocked.

"Because the police will take me away. Because my aunt Mildred will be coming for me."

Father Paul touched my arm gently. "I haven't told anyone about you, Kate. The two officers didn't ask who you were. I guessed because I was the one your minister called in order to locate your grandfather. I'm very sorry about your mother, Kate, and, I promise you, I've not revealed to anyone that you're here. I think you must tell your aunt soon, though."

"I will," I promised. "But I need a little more time."

"Do you really think you'd want to stay with Tsan if he'd have you?" Father Paul asked.

"I don't know," I admitted. "And anyway, I doubt I can convince Tsan to let me stay. But I definitely want time to get to know my grandfather."

"I think he should have the opportunity to get to know you too," Father Paul said as we walked back to the cabin. "Let's have a pact between us, Kate. You must let me call your aunt, to tell her that you are all right. In return, I'll do my best to convince her and Tsan that you should stay the summer. If they don't agree, I think you must abide by their wishes. But I can be very persuasive."

I thought about Father Paul's offer. It certainly couldn't hurt having him on my side. "Deal," I said, holding out my hand. Smiling, the priest gripped my hand firmly in his and shook it.

Nv?ya greeted our return with a whimper and came over to push his head between us when we sat down side by side on the floor in front of the fire. Tsan's deep, rythmic breathing made it clear that he was resting peacefully. While I scratched behind the German shepherd's ears, Father Paul and I talked about the poachers.

"It's unfortunate," the priest agreed, "but not uncommon in these mountains."

"Someone must be willing to pay a lot of money for the birds," I put in, "enough to make stealing them worth the effort and the risk. It's against the law isn't it?"

"Absolutely. And yes, I've heard that great sums are paid for the birds. I'm told that some Europeans, but especially certain people living in the Middle East, prize birds of prey. Hunting with them and even merely owning them is considered something which gives a man great prestige."

"But many of the birds must die, being treated so roughly. The ones I saw were stuffed into bags."

"It's all very cruel," Father Paul agreed.

"Tsan tried to stop them. He told me how much it bothered him to have the men steal the birds away from these mountains—their home. You only have to look at Tsan's pictures to see how much he loves the birds and other animals of the Snowbirds," I added, and I hurried to show Father Paul the stack of sketches I'd gathered up when we'd first returned to the cabin.

Father Paul appeared stunned. "I didn't know that Tsan was drawing again."

When I asked what he meant, he said, "I guess you should know, Kate, because this concerns you too."

A shiver rippled through me. I realized that I was going to learn the mystery, and I sat quietly, listening intently, as the priest told me the story.

"When Tsan was a young man, he loved to draw, and he proved himself talented enough to win a scholarship to the college which today has become Western Carolina University, in Cullohwee, North Carolina. There, he studied art and education. And while he was at the university, he met a white woman named Elizabeth Webb. They fell in love." Fresh goose bumps prickled my skin as I recognized my own middle name—Elizabeth.

"Upon graduation, Tsan returned to the Qualla Boundary to teach art at the high school. Although it was unusual for a white woman to do so, Elizabeth Webb also took a teaching position among the Cherokee. She taught at the elementary school and stayed with the family of one of her students. Just before Christmas of that year, she and Tsan were married.

"The people of the Qualla Boundary welcomed the young couple and shared their happiness. Elizabeth's family, however, strongly disapproved of the marriage. The Webbs, who lived in Asheville, North Carolina, were quite wealthy. Thomas Webb owned a textile mill and was a member of the city council. He and his wife were included socially when the Vanderbilts were in residence at their summer home, the Biltmore House. Prejudice still lingers against Native Americans, but in those days it was much worse. The Cherokee were disdained in the same way as blacks. So naturally, the Webbs felt that Elizabeth had made a disastrous mistake, and they refused to even meet her new husband.

"John and Elizabeth didn't care. They had each other, their jobs which gave them great pleasure, and a whole community of friends among the *Tsa la ki*. Three years later, they also had a son, Michael."

"Tsan told me his son died as a young child, so he couldn't be my father. Is that true?" I demanded.

"Sadly, to Tsan, it is," Father Paul said. "In actuality, though, it was Elizabeth who died. When Michael was thirteen, she developed tuberculosis, and when the doctor provided by the Agency could do nothing for her, Tsan swallowed his pride and sought help from the Webbs. They immediately agreed to put Elizabeth in a sanitarium near Asheville and to pay for the very best of care. The one requirement they made was that in return Tsan must allow them to care for Michael during the time that Elizabeth was undergoing treatment.

"The *Tsa la ki* believe that a man traces his lineage from his mother's clan. So this didn't seem an unreasonable request to Tsan. In fact, he felt it was a good thing, since Michael had never even met his mother's parents up until that time. I'm sure, for Elizabeth's sake, he also hoped that this gesture would help ease the strained conditions between the two families. And I know he felt sure his wife would recover quickly once she entered the sanitarium. The reputation of the doctors there was outstanding. Unfortunately, however, Elizabeth didn't respond to the treatment. She spent more than a year in the sanitarium, and then she died.

"Her death brought a terrible sadness to everyone on the Qualla Boundary because she was much loved. The grief became even greater when Tsan sought to bring his son home. The Webbs flatly refused, saying that they had custody and they intended to keep Michael. Tsan appealed to the courts for help. And after nearly a year of litigation, the judge finally ruled that since the boy had recently had his fifteenth birthday he was old enough to choose for himself.

"It was a terrible decision to force upon one so young, but it was his to make. Michael had already spent nearly three years with the Webbs by that time. Who's to say that he didn't choose them because he loved them. Tsan believed that it was because Michael wanted the things—the white man's things—that only his grandparents could provide. For whatever reason, Michael chose to remain with the Webbs.

"Tsan was crushed. He vowed that his son as well as his wife had died and, from that moment on, would have nothing to do with Michael. He also gave up teaching and removed himself from the community, building this cabin on the Snowbirds.

"I thought that he had also given up drawing and

83

painting—a way of cutting out everything that had been part of his past life. I'm glad to know that isn't true," Father Paul finished.

"My father never made an attempt to make up?" I wondered out loud.

"Yes, he did. He came once, just after he graduated from college. I met with him and directed him to Tsan, just as I did you," Father Paul remembered. "I had only recently returned home from the seminary myself at the time, and I believe—no, I know—there was a woman with him. It was undoubtedly your mother. They didn't stay long, though, and nothing changed with Tsan. So I assume father and son didn't make peace with each other."

"He should have tried harder," I blurted. "They both should have tried harder."

"I see your grandmother in you, Kate." The priest smiled. "Yes, I knew her well. You see, she was my fifth-grade teacher. Elizabeth Ridge was gentle but strong enough to risk a love that reached across two worlds— that of the *Ani: yo: wa ne: ka* and the *Ayv:wi yá hi*, the white people and the Indians."

"I'm not sure if I can be like her," I admitted. "I'm not even sure who I am yet."

Father Paul's laugh was a deep-throated boom. "Spoken as a truly liberated woman," he announced. "One thing is certain, Kate, what you accomplished today proved you have spirit—be it white or brown."

"Spirit, maybe," I replied, "but Tsan thinks I'm stupid. I don't seem to know the things he thinks are important. I don't even know how to speak any Cherokee."

"Ah, well, that's quickly remedied." Father Paul poked the fire, producing a burst of sparks and then added a new log to the crackling flames. "Do you know the hymn 'Jesus Loves Me'?"

"Of course."

"Good! Then sing it with me." Father Paul sat back down beside me and began to sing softly in a deep voice that was obviously used to leading songs. The melody was familiar, but the words—the Cherokee words—sounded strange. I sat listening quietly until, with a sweep of his hands, he motioned me to join in. Then I sang too, by repeating each phrase after him. When we'd sung the song once through this way, he began it again so we could sing the words together. And amazingly, this time the unfamiliar Cherokee words began to take shape and have meaning when fused with the familiar tune.

Tsis: sa a:ki ke: yú.
Jesus loves me.
koh wel a:khi no hi se.
Book   It tells me.
Tsu: nah sti ka Tsu: tse: li.
Little Ones   Belong to him.
U: hli ni: ki tih ye: hno.
Because he is strong.
Tsis   a:ki ke: yú.
Jesus   Loves me.
Tsis   a:ki ke: yú
Jesus   Loves me.
Tsis   a:ki ke: yú.
Jesus   Loves me.
akhi no hih se ho.
He tells me so.

Eleven

I awoke the next morning with a start and sat up quickly. At first, I felt confused by the surroundings and the disturbing dream images lingering in my mind. But the events of the day before quickly rushed back to me.

Father Paul had obviously already gotten up some time ago. The blankets he'd used to make a pallet for himself lay neatly folded in a stack on the floor beside me, and a fresh fire blazed in the fireplace. Its warmth felt good in the early morning chill that penetrated the small cabin. I turned, looking around for the priest, and when I didn't see him, I was suddenly afraid I'd slept so long that he'd already gone back down the mountain.

"A bad dream?" Tsan's question startled me. I hadn't realized he was awake, and now I saw that he was sitting up in his bed, sipping something from a mug. I wondered if Father Paul had made him more oak bark tea.

"Yes," I admitted. "Father Paul hasn't left already has he?"

Just then the cabin door opened, and Nv?ya bounded in ahead of the priest. "What a beautiful day for fishing. Early morning is the very best time for catching trout. Just look at these beauties." He proudly held up a string of four large, glistening brown fish with long snouts and rosy rainbow-hued streaks along their sides.

"So, Tsan, you're looking much better this morning. How about you, Kate? Did you sleep well?"

"Sure—except I had an awful nightmare. It was a lot like the one I had before," I told Tsan. "I'm in the eagle's nest. I don't really see the nest, but I'm sure that's where I am. Anyway, there are these two fluffy gray-brown birds right in front of me. They make the most pitiful peeping sound. It's almost a shriek. I want to help them by feeding them, only I don't have any food. I feel really bad because I don't have anything to give the baby birds. Then this one eaglet starts waddling toward me. I reach out for it, but before I can reach it, I slip and start to fall. That's when I always wake up."

"It's a vision," Tsan stated.

"But what does it mean?" I asked feeling puzzled and confused.

"Probably nothing," Father Paul put in.

"It's the eaglets' *a nih ski:na* calling. They haven't yet passed over into the Darkening Land," Tsan insisted.

"That's unlikely," Father Paul said, shaking his head. "Young eaglets must eat their own weight in food every day. I doubt if they've survived."

"It hasn't been all that long." I looked from Tsan to the priest. "Couldn't the eaglets still be alive?"

"It's unlikely," Father Paul repeated.

"It is possible," Tsan confirmed.

"Look, if there's a chance—any chance—I've got to find out for sure," I announced. I stood up so quickly that Nv?ya jumped to his feet, too, and barked, as though he understood that something exciting was happening.

"How can you?" Father Paul asked. "An eagle's nest is in the treetops."

"I'll climb up to it."

"It's too dangerous, Kate," Father Paul warned.

"I know. I dreamed about it. But I'll be really careful," I promised.

"It's too great a risk," he insisted.

Tsan, who had stayed out of the discussion up to this point, said suddenly, "*Ó sta tsi ki*—it is good! I feel sure it is what the *Nv: ne hi* want. It is why they have sent this girl a vision."

"Tsan, don't encourage her," Father Paul pleaded.

"Will you show me where the nest is, Tsan?" I asked.

"How could you not believe Kate is your granddaughter?" The priest spread his hands in a gesture of frustration. "See how stubborn she is."

Tsan looked at me as though he were seeing me for the first time. I felt uncomfortable under the intensity of his stare. At last he looked away as he pushed himself to his feet. "I will take you to the aerie," he said.

"Wait until after breakfast, at least," Father Paul demanded. "The mist still clings to the ground, and Kate needs the strength from a hearty breakfast."

I protested that I wasn't hungry and that the mist would surely be gone by the time we reached the eagle's nest. But the priest wouldn't yield on this point. And Tsan agreed that it was wise to wait a bit. So in the end,

I helped make breakfast, trying the best I could to hurry things along.

It seemed to take forever for Father Paul to clean the fish, for the fire to become hot enough in the stove, for the food to cook. In spite of myself, I found my stomach growling with anticipation as the trout sizzled in a bit of goat's milk butter in the iron skillet. The fish smelled delicious, and it tasted even better. Tsan said that Nv?ya was not to be spoiled with handouts, but I noticed that everyone—including Tsan—slipped the German shepherd tidbits of the flaky fish under the table.

After the plates had been washed and the fires in both the stove and the hearth had been banked, we were off. Tsan led the way, I followed, and Father Paul brought up the rear. Nv?ya was everywhere, bounding ahead and running back to lope along beside each of us in turn. I made a point of paying close attention to the woods this morning. I was determined to become familiar enough with this part of Snowbird Mountain to be able to venture away from the cabin on my own without getting lost. And to my surprise, I realized that I already recognized some landmarks, such as the rocky ridge Tsan and I had struggled up yesterday during our escape.

It was a long walk back to the logged-off area, and Tsan was noticeably tiring by the time we reached it. He sat down on a stump with a heavy sigh. "There," he said, pointing toward a tall old pine that stood just beyond the clearing.

I shaded my eyes from the sun with my hands and tipped my head back, scanning up, up, up the towering trunk. The nesting tree rose above the surrounding forest canopy. And high up, near the bristly crown, the eagle's nest looked like a pile of branches that had been blown by a strong wind and stuck in a messy bundle. Below, there were broad, spreading branches that extended down the trunk to within about fifteen feet of the ground. Only the stubby remains of old branches protruded on the lowest section of the trunk.

"It's too dangerous," Father Paul said, as he shaded his eyes to examine the impressively tall pine. "You can't climb that tree."

I licked my dry lips. "I think I can," I said.

"No," the priest insisted.

"I've been taking gymnastics since I was a little kid," I said. "I think I can do it. If it doesn't feel safe, I'll stop. I promise."

"Years of gymnastic training?" Father Paul repeated uncertainly. "I don't know. What do you think, Tsan?"

The Indian's expression revealed nothing of his thoughts. He said only, "I've brought you to the aerie as I promised."

Before Father Paul could insist and before I lost my nerve, I made a dash for the pine's trunk. Letting my momentum help boost me, the way I'd been taught to mount the parallel bars, I leapt, reaching up for the lowest limb. I caught the short stubby projection with both hands, then swung my body up, planting both feet on the limb, and straightened, reaching immediately for the next higher branch.

"Kate, be careful," Father Paul called.

"This is a lot easier than walking down that ledge," I answered, wiping my sweaty hands on my jeans.

"What ledge?" the priest asked. Tsan didn't answer. I didn't either. I was too busy climbing.

At first, I counted the branches, thinking this would help me know how I was doing on the way back down.

But eventually, I lost count. Instead, I started looking up, feeling encouraged as the distance between myself and the base of the nest shrank.

Climbing was hard work. My muscles—from my arms through my stomach and all down my legs—ached from the strain of repeatedly lifting my weight to the next higher branch. My hands were also sore from gripping the rough pine boughs. The morning air was still crisply cool, but I was sweating from my effort and my windbreaker was starting to stick to my arms. I left the jacket on, though. If any of the eaglets was alive, I could tuck the little baby birds into my jacket pouch and keep both hands free on my return trip.

Were the eaglets alive? I listened hard, hoping to hear the plaintive peeps that haunted my dreams. All I heard was the wind rustling through the needle-covered branches and occasionally Nv?ya's sharp barks.

My muscles quivered from the strain as I pulled myself up yet another level. *I could be putting myself through this for nothing,* I thought. Then I reminded myself that this risk wasn't *for nothing.* It was for the eaglets. There was a chance they were still alive, and I had to find out.

Boy, I thought, *if Chrissy could see me now, she'd think I was crazy! And Aunt Mildred—she'd have a fit.* I thought about my mom, too, and what she would say if she knew I was here, with Tsan, trying to save eaglets from poachers. I was sure she'd think I was doing the right thing. In fact, I bet she'd be proud of me.

I had been concentrating so hard on pulling myself up from limb to limb that I was surprised when I finally found myself just below the base of the nest. Now I was faced with a new challenge. As big as the aerie was, I had no doubt it would support my weight once I was on top of it. The problem was going to be getting up the side. Sticks as big around as a man's arm had somehow been piled and woven together to create this giant nest. Its depth was greater than my height. So I wasn't going to be able to reach the top edge of the nest with one grasp. I was going to have to climb up the side of the nest.

I leaned against the rough trunk of the ancient pine, looked down through its spreading branches, and swallowed against the tightness constricting my throat. As awesome as the challenge of climbing the pine had been, this was more formidable. And I was afraid.

I stood perched below the eagles' nest for a few seconds, a few minutes, maybe longer—listening. The wind played a whispery tune on the long pine needles, but I didn't hear the eaglets' cries I'd hoped for. I'd about decided that maybe it wasn't worth the additional effort and risk to tackle the nest when Father Paul called to me.

"I'm all right," I hollered down through the wind and the branches. "I'm . . ." I started to tell him I was coming back down when I heard a shrill noise. Had it come from the nest? Or had it only been the wind?

"Hello?" I called, for a lack of knowing what else to say. My call was immediately echoed by another shrill shriek. The sound had definitely come from the nest above me.

I reached up with one hand and then the other, scraping my knuckles as I thrust my fingers into the jumble, anchoring my hold on the nest. I pulled, straining, slowly hoisting my weight. The moment I pulled my feet up on the nest was especially scary because now there was no base support I could trust. Some of the smaller, brittle twigs cracked as the rubber soles of my sneakers pushed against them. Sweating, breathing hard, I reached my right hand up again and caught the lip of the nest.

Suddenly, I felt a sharp pain in my right hand. Something had jabbed me. I fought the instinctive urge to jerk my hand away from the pain and hung on. A second jab shot a lighting bolt coursing up my arm. Then I realized what was happening. An eaglet was attacking me. The poor baby bird desperately wanted help, but it didn't want it from me.

I reached my left hand up and grabbed the edge of the nest. Then, with a burst of energy I was surprised I had left, I propelled myself up over the edge of the nest and face to face with a big ugly monster.

This was no cute little fuzzy baby bird. In fact, it was hard to even imagine that this ugly creature could ever become a beautiful adult eagle. The fledgling was black, with a body about the size of a football, and sticking up from this was a long scrawny neck topped by a rather small head. The eaglet watched me with shiny, jet-black eyes. Its hooked beak was open; its large toes, ending in curving, sharp-tipped talons, were thrust out across the grass lining of the nest; and its big wings were fully spread. I had no doubt that this pose was meant to scare me away. The eaglet was so silly-looking, though, that it was impossible to be frightened. The mix of gray down and sleek black feathers gave the fledgling a ragged scarecrow appearance. Its flight feathers were just starting to grow in, so its wings were edged with what looked like dangling, feather-tipped straws.

"You're going to have to finish growing up to be impressive," I informed the eaglet.

"*Kek-kek-kek,*" it shrieked at me. Then it jerked its head forward. I only barely managed to avoid having my hand nipped again.

"C'mon. Give me a break," I pleaded. "I'm here to save you. Try to act like you appreciate me at least a little bit."

"*Kek-kek-kek,*" the eaglet repeated.

"Okay. I guess you've got a right to be upset. But I have to figure out a way to get us both down to the ground safely. You're an awful lot bigger than I dreamed," I told the bird. The eaglet answered me with a shriek and another attempt to take a chunk out of me—my leg this time.

Just then Nv?ya barked loudly. Even though the German shepherd's bark was greatly diminished by distance, the eaglet was obviously startled by these threatening sounds. The bird immediately folded its wings and hunkered down among the dry grass.

"Hey, that's more like it," I announced. "You know, if you stay like that you might actually fit in my jacket pouch." I unzipped the pouch in the front of my windbreaker and reached for the eaglet. But I stopped then, remembering my dream. This was the point at which I always fell. I felt suddenly hot and cold at the same time. My heart began to pound. Was that the omen? Had my dream been a warning vision of something that was going to happen to *me*?

No. That was silly. Dreams were just dreams. They weren't really *visions*.

I scooped up the young bird and stuffed it into my jacket pouch. That was when I saw the remains of another eaglet. I realized that eating part of its nestmate was probably what had kept this young bird alive. I felt oddly queasy for a few seconds, but I reminded myself that this was survival of the fittest. At least one fledgling was still alive.

The eaglet had its head poking out of my jacket pouch, and it recovered from its momentary meekness enough to make protesting shrieks and struggle to escape. My windbreaker appeared to take on a life of its own as the bird wriggled and thrashed, and I felt the eaglet's sharp talons pierce my sweatshirt and prick my skin.

"Cut it out," I ordered, but the eaglet continued to struggle. Then, with sudden inspiration, I barked loudly, imitating Nv?ya. The eaglet was instantly still.

"Hey! Pretty clever." I grinned. While the eaglet was subdued, I gently pushed its head inside the pouch and zipped it shut. Then I hurriedly slipped my legs over the edge of the nest and began lowering myself down the side. My left foot found a branch to stand on, and my right foot followed. Whenever the eaglet wiggled, I barked until it was still, all the while steadily lowering myself from branch to branch.

The ground was coming closer, but, oh so slowly. My leg muscles began to quiver with fatigue. I don't know if it was a muscle cramp that made my foot jerk or if I just misstepped. But suddenly, I was clinging to a branch while my legs dangled free. I kicked the air, trying to get at least one foot back on the branch below me.

It took several tries, but when my foot finally found the branch, I stood on it leaning back against the pine tree's trunk. It seemed comforting to have the support of something solid. Then the eaglet stirred. I had started to bark again when I heard a crack, and my voice just stuck in my throat. Desperately, I reached up for the branch directly above me. But I wasn't fast enough.

I was falling.

Down.

Down.

Down.

It was just the way I had experienced it in my dream.

Twelve

I clawed wildly for the branches flying by me, but I couldn't seem to grab one. Then a big branch whomped against my back driving the wind out of me, but it seemed to slow me too. As if by some miracle, my hands locked around the rough limb, and for a few wonderful seconds I hung suspended as if from a trapeze. Then this branch snapped, too, and I started to fall once again.

It was the ground that finally stopped me. Luckily the last drop had only been about ten feet, and I landed on my back on the pine-straw cushion that the tree had piled up at its base.

"Kate. Oh, my goodness, Kate. Are you all right?" Father Paul cried, as he, Tsan, and Nv?ya rushed to my aid. Although I felt stunned, nothing seemed to be broken. I struggled to sit up.

"No. Lie still a minute," Tsan told me. "Let your spirit catch up to your body."

I lay back with a sigh, deciding he was right. I needed to catch my breath. Then as I lay there on the pine straw, my chest began to bulge bigger and bigger. It felt weird, and it looked even weirder.

"Oooh," I groaned.

"Kate? What is it?" Father Paul demanded.

Suddenly my nylon jacket tore, and as everyone stared, the eaglet poked its black head out and nipped Father Paul's hand.

"Ouch!" The priest jerked back. Nv?ya barked a noisy protest. And the eaglet glared open-beaked at the dog. Tsan reached over me and firmly but gently pressed the young bird's beak closed with his fingers.

"Shhhh, little one," the old man crooned. I lay still as Tsan proceeded to ease the bird's wings out through the hole in my jacket. Then he stood up, cradling the strange-looking black bird in his arms. Father Paul helped me up.

"You're really all right?" the priest asked.

"Yes. I think so." I wiggled my shoulders and moved various parts to reassure myself. "It was just like my nightmare," I reported.

"But you're okay," Father Paul made it a statement this time. "Thanks be to God."

"What are we going to do for him ... her?" I pointed at the bird.

"By the size of it, I'd say it's a female," Tsan explained. "Female bald eagles are always bigger than the males. I'm going to take her home. I have a cage that will hold her until she calms down and gets used to being around people. You two are going fishing so we'll have something to feed this poor creature. She must be starved!"

I almost said something about the other eaglet, the

one whose remains had sustained this one, but I didn't. I didn't want to spoil what felt like a happy moment with that sad news.

"You're going to need someone to catch fish for the eaglet every day," Father Paul said, falling into step beside Tsan, while Nv?ya and I followed along behind them.

"Umpf," grunted Tsan. I wasn't sure what that meant, but it hadn't sounded very positive.

"You're going to need someone to take the goats out to pasture, feed the chickens, carry water, and hoe the garden too," Father Paul continued. "Kate wants to stay with you for the summer. She's promised to go back to her aunt at the end of that time. This would give your shoulder time to heal. And I think she could really be a big help to you—especially now."

I held my breath expecting Tsan to protest. But to my surprise, he consented without even putting up an argument. "I can stay?" I asked.

"Only until school starts," Tsan repeated casting a look at me over his shoulder. "But she will have to work hard and learn a lot if she is going to be of any use," he told the priest.

"To hi yu—true," Father Paul agreed. "But you are a good teacher, Tsan. You can instruct Kate in the *Tsa la ki* way." I was beaming as the priest tossed me a wink. "What do you say, Kate?"

"Ó sta tsi ki—it is good!" I announced, trying out one of the Cherokee words Father Paul had taught me last night.

Tsan stopped and turned around to look at me. He corrected my pronunciation, but he didn't seem angry. In fact, I could have sworn he almost smiled. Almost.

"Tell me one thing," he said. "I have been most curious as to why you have your teeth wired into your mouth. Are they so very loose?"

I was too surprised to speak, as Father Paul's deep booming laugh filled the air. "No. No, my good friend," he said, when he'd recovered. "This is something that is even being done to *Tsa la ki* children these days. If you came down into the village once in a while, you'd know that."

"The wires are called braces, and they're going to make my teeth straight," I explained. Tsan only shook his head, as if in wonder at such an idea, and continued on his way toward his house.

Tsan took the priest at his word about my instruction, and my lessons began that very day, as he taught me how to scale the fish Father Paul and I caught for the eaglet and for our own dinner. Scaling was something I didn't enjoy very much, and I didn't do it very well that first time. Father Paul seemed to find the way I splattered fish scales all over myself very amusing.

The lessons went on every day, from the instant I got up in the morning until the moment I lay down to go to sleep at night. I didn't mind, though, because it wasn't like going to school. A lot of what Tsan taught me were things I needed to know in order to be helpful. For example, I learned how to collect eggs from chickens without being pecked and how to herd goats so they'll go in the direction you want. Both are a lot trickier to do than they sound. And I learned how to use a *kha no: na*—a mortar—to pound corn so it becomes meal of just the right fineness for preparing porridge, bread, or *ka no he: na*—a kind of sour corn gruel, which tastes surprisingly good.

Even long walks, which we often took, became lessons, as Tsan pointed out animals, showed me their tracks, or called my attention to the sounds they made. He taught me to identify plants, too, and told me how they could be used.

"There's the willow," he'd say. "Like the oak, its bark can be made into tea that helps stop pain. It's not as good as the oak, though, when there's a wound."

"You have to remember goldenrod," he told me, grasping one of the big plants where it emerged from the ground and gently tugging its roots free. "See these bright yellow flowers? That's how you'll know it. A tea made from those flowers can be counted on to take away fever. For some it's good for bladder problems—but only for some. Be sure to collect the goldenrod root, too, because you can make a tea from that to cure a cold. And if someone has a toothache, chewing on the root is certain to relieve the pain."

Tsan gave me frequent quizzes to make sure I really learned my lessons. He'd stop suddenly while we were walking, point to a set of tracks, and ask what animal had been there ahead of us. Or he'd point to a plant I'd barely had time to notice and demand, "What is this one? How can you use it?"

Father Paul came back at the end of my first week on Snowbird Mountain to report that he'd spoken to Aunt Mildred. He said that she'd been both furious and frantic with worry and that she had agreed to consider letting me stay. She wanted to see me first, however. She was, in fact, coming the next day. To make it easier for her, and because Father Paul knew Tsan would resent having visitors, the priest explained that I was to go into town with him in the morning. My nervousness over the prospect of facing my aunt must have shown, because Father Paul quickly assured me that he would stay with me during the visit.

Then, to prove how much I'd learned in the past week, I prepared dinner all by myself. I split the wood for the stove. I stewed the rabbit Tsan had trapped and skinned, with carrots and wild potatoes, which aren't really potatoes but the tasty potatolike tuber roots of the arrowhead plant. I didn't think I could ever eat rabbit, but I knew that this, too, was part of life on Snowbird Mountain, where even eating was a matter of survival. For dessert, I had picked blueberries from the bushes near the creek, and I served these in bowls with a little of Tsan's maple syrup drizzled over the top.

"Wonderful, Kate." Father Paul praised my efforts. "I wish your aunt could see how well you're doing."

I smiled. "Josie and Becca—my cousins—would have been crazy about the blueberries," I said. "But if they'd picked them, there wouldn't have been enough for the rest of us."

Father Paul laughed. "Then it's a good thing Josie and Becca aren't here, because I wouldn't have wanted to give up my share. There's nothing quite as delicious as the blueberries that grow in these mountains."

"Mmm," Tsan grunted his agreement. "Blueberries have always been one of my favorite fruits."

"Wasn't it my father's favorite too?" I asked.

Tsan's expression instantly became stormy. "I don't remember," he said.

"Yes, you do," I snapped. "You're just too stubborn to admit you remember anything about my father."

Tsan glowered at me, and Father Paul gently patted my arm, but I ignored his warning to stop. "I don't know why my father chose to live with his grandparents instead of with you," I said, "but there has to have been something good—some happy time—that you remember about him."

Tsan pushed himself to his feet. "Enough! I don't want to talk about Michael."

I stood up, meeting his angry gaze. "But I do. I want to know more about my father. He's partly the reason why I came here, why I wanted to get to know you. And I think you were wrong for never making up with him."

"How dare you talk to me like that," Tsan thundered. "I never should have let you stay. Get out."

Father Paul was on his feet now too. "No. Tsan. You don't mean that."

But he did. I knew he did. I felt hot tears spring to my eyes, and I ran out of the cabin.

Nv?ya leapt from his favorite spot on the bench next to the door and bounded down the steps at my heels.

"Stay," I ordered. But Nv?ya didn't obey me, and when I reached the woods, I stopped, swung around to face the dog, and pointed back toward the cabin. "Go back, you silly mutt," I yelled. "Can't you tell when you're not wanted?"

Nvya cocked his head to one side, regarded me with sad-looking big, brown eyes, and whined.

"I'm sorry," I said, wiping away the tears that were spilling onto my cheeks. "It's just that ... that ..." Unable to find any words that expressed the hurt and frustration I felt, I turned and plunged into the forest, following the now familiar path that led to the creek. I just wanted to be alone. Funny that not so very long ago the idea of being alone on Snowbird Mountain at night had terrified me.

When I came to the boulder that juts out over the creek, I stretched out on it and peered down into the water. The moonlight made the surface a shimmering mirror cut into oddly shaped pieces by the trees' black shadows. My own reflection added a bump to the boulder's shadow. Farther out from the shore, the moon's reflection was a dazzling disk that shattered into a million pieces when a fish jumped.

Suddenly, I felt more than alone. I felt lonely. "I miss you, Chrissy," I told the shadow of my reflection in the water. "I'm so confused. What am I going to do now?"

I thought about my best friend, the times we'd shared. "I wish things could just be the way they used to," I said. "I wish we could just hang out in my room, play music, eat Mom's brownies, and talk about all this."

Did Tsan really mean what he'd said? Was I really going to have to leave tomorrow? I was sorry about what I'd said and that I'd let my temper get out of control, but I was also still angry at Tsan. That he could still be so resentful after all these years just didn't make any sense.

I was so wrapped up in my own thoughts that I didn't hear the noise. The fish jumping finally caught my attention, and I noticed the soft thunking sound coming from the woods downstream. There was a pause in the rhythmic thunks broken only by a cicada booming its mating call. Then I heard more clunks and thumps.

Could it be an animal? Tsan had taught me about the *tho: tsuh wa*—the redbird; the *to: yi*—the beaver; the *ah wi*—the deer; and *ka: kal ka nv hi ta*—a kind of bear that he'd called Long Hams.

The *bear*! I eased backward off the boulder, landed in a crouch, and stayed down on my hands and knees in the shadows. As quickly as I could, I crawled away from the stream until I reached the trees. Then I stood up, pressed my back against the trunk of a tall old oak, and stayed very still—listening.

I was sure I heard breathing. Something—maybe Long Hams—was on the other side of this tree trunk.

Thirteen

For a long moment, fear held my feet anchored to the ground. Then I made a run for it. But at the very instant I burst into action, a solid shape swung in front of me, and we crashed.

"Oof!" came a startled cry as hands tightly gripped both of my arms just below the shoulders.

I lifted my head and looked into the angry face of a young girl who was slightly taller and appeared to be a little older than I was. With a toss of her head she flipped back long hair that was so brilliantly copper-hued that even the darkness couldn't dim its fiery shade.

"You scared me to death," the girl accused. "Why were you sneaking up on me?"

"I ... I ... I wasn't," I sputtered.

"Don't try to deny it." She released my shoulders and put her hands on her hips. "I saw you crawling across the ground. That's sneaking if I ever saw it."

"No, it isn't. I mean, I wasn't. Honest. I was trying to get away. I thought you were Long Hams."

"The bear?" She sounded amused, and she leaned closer, peering into my face. Even though it was dark, I could tell that her eyes were fair and not jet black as I'd come to expect of the Cherokee. I was wondering who she was and what she was doing up here on Snowbird Mountain when she asked me the same thing.

"I'm Kate Ridge," I told her. "My grandfather's house is close to here, and I ... I went for a walk," I added.

"Your Tsan's granddaughter? Really?" Now she sounded impressed.

"Yes. But why are you out here on the mountain in the dark?" I asked. "Are you lost?"

The girl's smile flashed even, white teeth. "No, I'm not lost. I'm Dorothy Standingdeer. My grandparents live over there—beyond that ridge. I've been staying with them." She pointed. Then her face wrinkled in a frown. "You didn't see what I was doing, did you?" she demanded.

"No," I assured her, instantly wondering what she *had* been doing.

"Oh, I didn't mean to sound so secretive. It's just that I've been tending my *tso: la ka yv: li*, and you know that all its magic would be lost if anyone saw it growing."

"Your what?" I asked.

Dorothy looked suspicious again. "You're Tsan's granddaughter and you don't know about *tso: la ka yv: li*?"

I replied that I'd only recently found my grandfather and that until that time I'd spent my whole life among the *ani: yo: wa ne: ka*—the white people. This seemed to satisfy her and she explained that *tso: la ka yv: li* is wild tobacco that's grown to work magic.

"Some people think it's just as good to use a pinch of pipe tobacco," she added. "But I'm not going to take any chances. This is too important. The magic has to be absolutely right." Dorothy leaned close and whispered, "You see, I've been in love with Calhoun Chilkowsky for years now, but he's never even noticed me.

"That's about to change, though," she continued. "I'm going to make sure that at the end of the summer when Calhoun sees me at the Green Corn Festival he'll not only notice me, he won't be able to forget me. You really didn't see me cultivating the *tso: la ka yv: li*, did you? It would spoil everything if you had."

"No. I didn't. I promise."

Dorothy sighed. "I've gone to a lot of trouble to make this batch perfect. First, I burned lightning-struck wood on the plot. Then I waited to plant until a storm so there would be thunder while I was putting the seeds in the ground. Now the tobacco is almost ready for your grandfather to *koh sv hih sah nv hi–tso: la*—to remake it. He knows the words that must be said over the *tso: la ka yv: li* to give it power, how to mix it with other tobacco to make the potion, and how to sprinkle the potion to deliver the spell that will make me unforgettable enough to win Calhoun's heart."

"Why do you have to use tobacco?" I asked.

Dorothy thought about this for a minute. "That's just the way it's always been done. There are a lot of spells for things like making it rain, saving a corn crop that's been blown over by the wind, catching fish, or getting rid of bad luck, and most of these require the use of tobacco. Some people say these are just superstitions, but many people use these spells all the same."

"Tell me about Calhoun," I urged, as we walked back down to the creek and sat down side by side on the boulder.

"He's wonderful!" Dorothy exclaimed. "He's strong and tall—almost a head taller than I am—and kind and clever and very handsome." She paused, then asked, "Tell me how you came to be with Tsan?" And so, as briefly as I could, I told her my story, about my mom, and how I'd found my grandfather with Father Paul's help.

"I can't believe you ran away," Dorothy said. "I mean, how come you want to live up here on the mountain? Tsan doesn't have a television or even an indoor bathroom. I'm sure Cherokee doesn't have a lot of the things that Atlanta has, but at least in town there are indoor toilets, running water, and televisions."

"Oh, sure, I miss those things," I said, "but do you know what I really miss?"

Dorothy shook her head.

"I miss being able to call my friends, especially Chrissy. She's my best friend."

Dorothy laughed. "My mother says the phone is going to become permanently attached to my ear because I talk on it so much."

"My mother used to say that too!" I exclaimed. Then, because she seemed so much like me, I asked, "Are you full-blooded Cherokee?"

"Of course I am." Dorothy sounded offended, but before I could apologize she giggled. "Oh, you mean on account of my red hair and hazel eyes. Well, technically,

I suppose I'm not. You see when pioneers used to cross these mountains on their way west they'd sometimes stop in the valley. The *Tsa la ki* were always friendly, giving them food and water—helping out any way they could.

"Now and then when a mother died or something happened to both parents, a *Tsa la ki* family would even take in a child and raise it as one of their own. Later, when the first census takers came to the Qualla Boundary and asked if these rather different-looking children were theirs, they naturally answered yes. So the white children officially became full-blooded *Tsa la ki* and their non-Cherokee traits just keep popping up. Like in me." Dorothy stood and said, "It's getting late. I'd better go before my grandparents start to worry."

"Will you come to Tsan's to visit me?" I asked. Now that I'd found a friend, I realized how much I'd missed having someone my own age to talk to. I was anxious to see Dorothy again.

"Yes. I'll come tomorrow afternoon," she promised. She was gone before I remembered to tell her that I might not be here tomorrow afternoon.

When I got back to the cabin, Tsan was waiting for me on the porch bench with Nv?ya lying at his feet. He had a kerosene lantern beside him, and he was whittling by its yellowish light. His knobby fingers moved with surprising swiftness as tiny flecks of wood flew away from his knife. When I was close enough, I could see that he was carving a likeness of the German shepherd. He stopped, looking up at me as I climbed the porch steps.

"I thought I might have to send Nv?ya to find you," Tsan said gruffly.

My stomach did a somersault. Had he actually been worried that I might not come back? "I was down at the stream," I said. "I met Dorothy Standingdeer, and we started talking."

"I know Dorothy," Tsan reported, with a nod that I took to be approval of my new friend. We were silent for a few long minutes, looking at each other across the darkness. Then Tsan began whittling again, adding texture to the wooden dog's furry coat with quick, short knife strokes. I struggled to think of a way to explain to my grandfather that I was sorry for what had happened between us earlier but not for what I'd said. When Tsan continued to whittle in silence and I couldn't seem to find the right words, I gave up and started toward the cabin door.

"The winter Michael was twelve," Tsan began softly.

"Excuse me?" I said, stopping and turning back toward him.

"When Michael was twelve," Tsan repeated more loudly, "Mary Thomas, an old woman who lived up here on Snowbird Mountain, fell and broke her hip. The doctor wanted a helicopter to come and take her to the hospital—" He gestured to show it was a long ways away. "—the one that lies beyond the Qualla Boundary. But Mary didn't want to leave. This was her home, the house of her mother's family. Before that, her people had lived in the cave below the ridge, so they had always lived on Snowbird Mountain."

"They lived in that cave?" I asked.

"Many of the *Tsa la ki* hid in caves when the white men came to force them from their homeland, and they were forced to go on hiding for a number of years.

"Michael loved Mary like a grandmother. He used to

visit her and she'd always bake special treats for him, so when she was injured he wanted to help her. Michael promised Dr. Lamb that he would help take care of Mary so she could remain in her home. We were living in town then, so he moved in with Mary and did all the chores. When school started, he hiked down to the road to catch the bus every morning. Michael lived up here on the mountain for four months until Mary was able to take care of herself.

"It was a lot of work for a young boy," Tsan added, as his hands stopped and he held the finished figure of Nvya out to me. "But Michael did the job well."

I accepted the gift Tsan offered me, swallowing against the tightness in my throat. "*Wa tó*—thanks," I said. "I ... I ..."

"Get some sleep," Tsan said. "You have a lot to do tomorrow. When you get back from seeing your aunt, we need to start tanning the rabbit pelts. Go on now. I'll be along as soon as I check the gate on the goat yard."

"*Ha yu*—yes, sir." My hopes soared with the knowledge that Tsan had plans for me—that I could stay for the summer if my aunt would let me. I quickly gave Nv?ya's head a pat, and then I tiptoed into the cabin, being quiet so I wouldn't wake Father Paul. My mattress of cotton ticking stuffed with sweet-smelling meadow grass was already laid out near the hearth. Once I'd put on my nightgown in the corner of the kitchen I used as a dressing area, I slipped under the patchwork quilt and set the wooden dog down beside my bed. There in the flickering shadows, it seemed to take on a life of its own, and watching it, I thought about my father. I remembered what he'd looked like in the pictures I'd seen and tried to imagine him as a boy, fishing, trapping rabbits, and herding goats in the high mountain meadow just as I was now doing.

My mother always said my imagination worked overtime, and I started to think about what it would be like to stay with Tsan and Nv?ya and the eaglet on Snowbird Mountain this winter. I imagined myself playing in the snow with Nv?ya. I could picture the deep drifts of clean, white mountain snow, unlike any snowfall I'd ever seen in Atlanta. At the end of the winter there would be the three springs that Tsan had told me about—the mountain laurel spring, the rhododendron spring, and the dogwood spring—each with its own beautiful display of new wildflowers.

I looked at the carved figure of Nv?ya he'd given me and felt fresh hope that we could be friends. But I was afraid to ask Tsan if I could stay. It seemed pretty unlikely he'd want to have a kid around on a permanent basis—even one that had gotten pretty good at chopping wood and a lot of other things. I was afraid to mention my idea about staying longer than this summer to Father Paul too. Just wanting to be here didn't seem nearly reason enough. Only, I couldn't seem to come up with any other at the moment. It was something I would have to work on. Of course, first, I had to convince Aunt Mildred to let me stay for the summer.

Fourteen

Aunt Mildred was sitting on a wooden bench under the sweeping overhanging roof of the Qualla Arts and Crafts building when Father Paul and I arrived just after ten. She'd obviously already been inside the gift shop, because two bulging green paper bags were sitting at her feet. She looked exhausted even though it was still early in the day.

"I can't begin to tell you the trouble you caused your uncle and me," she said.

"I'm sorry," I answered.

"When is your baby due?" Father Paul asked, after introducing himself to my aunt. There was no question that the due date had to be imminent. Before she could answer, though, Josie and Becca pushed through the big wooden doors of the building together.

"Mama, come buy me that Indian doll, pleeeee—ease," Josie begged.

Becca's expression was scrunched agony. "You promised it to me. You promised, Mommy."

As the girls engulfed their mother and their pleas increased in volume, Chrissy emerged from the store.

"Chrissy!" I called in delight.

We ran over to each other and hugged. Then we both began talking at once.

"I was hoping I'd at least get to call you," I said.

"I just had to know if you were all right," she said. "So I offered to help with the girls if your aunt would let me come along. What a job!" She rolled her eyes and we both laughed.

"I've missed you."

"I've missed you too. I didn't tell them where you were," Chrissy reported proudly.

"I knew you wouldn't," I told her. "Was your mom mad about the money?"

"She was really understanding, Kate. She wanted me to tell you not to worry about paying her back. She was pretty upset that you ran away, though, and that I helped you do it. Everybody was *really* upset about that. Your aunt most of all. She called the police, the lawyer, the Reverend Maxwell. She kept saying what a lot of trouble you were and that she didn't know how she was ever going to handle you."

Handle me. The words stung. I pinched my lower lip between my teeth and looked at Aunt Mildred who was red in the face and waving her arms as she struggled to *handle* her daughters.

"Perhaps there are two identical dolls," Father Paul suggested loudly enough to be heard over Josie's and Becca's cries.

"Pleeeee-ease, Mama," Josie pleaded.

"I want the dolly," Becca wailed.

"Yes, two dolls," Aunt Mildred said. My cousins shrieked with delight and ran back into the store as she plucked her billfold from her purse and gave it to Chrissy. "The girls are just too much for me today," she added.

Chrissy rolled her eyes at me again before she followed the girls.

"They're very energetic," Father Paul commented.

Aunt Mildred looked at him sharply. "As you can see this is an especially difficult time for me."

"Of course." Father Paul sat down beside her. "When is the baby due?"

"Next month," Aunt Mildred answered, and then she pointed a finger at me. "You can't imagine how much trouble *you've* caused me."

"I didn't think ..."

"No, you never do," she snapped.

"Under the circumstances, Kate's curiosity about her grandfather was only ..." Father Paul began.

"This is strictly a family matter," Aunt Mildred interrupted. She pointed her finger at me again. "I thought you were going to be a big help to me. Now I can see that you're just going to be one more kid that I'm going to have to deal with. Lord knows, I've got my hands full already."

"Indeed he does," Father Paul said, smiling, and Aunt Mildred tossed him another icy look.

"Well, I can't take on any more responsibility right now. I can see that she's doing all right. So I think that if her grandfather is willing to have Kate stay for the rest of the summer, maybe that's for the best. I've talked to the lawyer, and he doesn't feel this arrangement will jeopardize the trust at all. Father, if it's all right with you, I'll send a box with the things I think Kate will need—and a *small* allowance that Mr. Wescott, the lawyer, recommended."

"Of course," Father Paul answered.

"Wa tó," I said, barely able to restrain the urge to jump up and down with joy.

"Wa tó? What kind of talk is that?"

"I mean, thank you," I said, feeling color rush hot to my cheeks.

"If my niece is learning some kind of foreign tongue here ..." Aunt Mildred fumed, but she was interrupted by Josie and Becca, who reappeared and rushed to show her their purchases.

"Oh, my God, look at the price of these dolls!" she shrieked. "They're going back right now."

"No. I love my dolly," Becca wailed, and Josie began to sob.

"Frank?" Aunt Mildred called. "Frank, I need you." Aunt Mildred and the girls went back into the Qualla Arts and Crafts building as Chrissy came out.

"I can't believe it, Chrissy. My aunt's letting me stay!"

"That's great." We hugged again. "But I'm really going to miss you, Kate," she added.

We had only a few more minutes to talk before Aunt Mildred and the girls returned. This time Uncle Frank was with them, and he quickly ushered everyone into the family's station wagon.

"Write me," Chrissy called, leaning out the window.

"I will," I promised. I kept waving until the car was out of sight.

"Well, well," Father Paul said as we walked back to his Jeep.

"My mother wasn't anything like Aunt Mildred," I told him.

"Knowing you, I didn't think she was," he said, and we both smiled. Then he looked at his watch "I have a couple of things to do before I can drive you back to Tsan's. I could leave you here. The Cherokee Heritage Museum is that building just across the parking lot, if you'd like to look around."

I opted to go along with him and save the museum tour for another day. Our first stop was at a line of small shops nestled on the side of the mountain that rose behind a sprawling complex of buildings. Father Paul explained that this complex was the school for the Qualla Boundary—kindergarten through high school. We went into a small shop next to the credit union. It wasn't really a store. It was a place where people could get free books, and it was only open when a load of books arrived. Several young children were there with their mother, selecting one book each. Father Paul spoke to the young Cherokee woman who was in charge, then picked up a box she pointed out to him and loaded it into the Jeep.

"For the library," he told me.

We drove back past the Cherokee museum and Qualla Arts and Crafts building, across a narrow bridge spanning the Oconoluftee River, and down a winding two-lane road to what looked like another school building. This, Father Paul explained, was the community recreation center. The library was in a room in the back of this building.

"Hello, Father Paul," a voice called as we passed one of the many small offices along the hall.

"Well, Sam Youngbird. How goes your summer?"

When I turned around to see who Father Paul was talking to, I found myself gazing into the biggest brown eyes I'd ever seen. "This is Kate Ridge." I heard myself being introduced, but I couldn't seem to stop staring. "She's staying with her grandfather up on Snowbird Mountain."

"Nice to meet you," Sam flashed a smile that lit up his whole face. "You going to go to school here this fall?"

"I ... I ..."

"Kate's plans are a little uncertain right now, but she'll definitely be around for the rest of the summer."

Sam nodded, still smiling. "Maybe I'll see you around."

I smiled too. It was impossible not to; his smile was contagious.

When Sam had gone, Father Paul reported, "Good student, ninth grader, plays on the baseball team. There are a lot of activities going on here at the center and always a lot of young people around." As if to prove his point, two girls came toward us down the hall, and he introduced me to Wanda Hatfield and Marcia Ax. Wanda was a year older than I am, but Marcia was my age, and they both seemed very nice. They were on their way to a pottery class.

"You'll have to come into town one of these days," Father Paul suggested. "Spend some time at the center and get to know some of the young people—maybe when there's a baseball game."

I thought that sounded like a very good idea, and I made a mental note to ask Dorothy if she knew Sam Youngbird, and if so, what he was like. Then Father Paul took me to lunch at the same restaurant where I'd stopped the first day I'd arrived in Cherokee. We both had cheeseburgers and Cokes, and for dessert, we had hot fudge sundaes. Before we left the village, I decided to splurge and do a little shopping since Aunt Mildred had promised to send an allowance. I bought a sketch pad and some colored pencils for myself and a bag of hard fruit-flavored candies with soft centers for Tsan.

Father Paul had church duties to attend to that evening, so he drove me up Snowbird Mountain only as far as the fork in the trail, and I walked from there. I came upon Tsan as I was crossing the high meadow.

"Hey, hey," I called, shooing a straying goat back toward the herd. Nv?ya, having rounded up another straggler, fell in beside me, nipping at the goat's heels to keep her headed in the right direction.

"It was getting late," Tsan said when I caught up with him. "I thought you'd gone with your aunt."

"You can't get rid of me that easily," I said.

"Umpf," Tsan grunted, but I thought he looked pleased to see me all the same. "If you're going to stay for rest of the summer," he added, "you're going to have to work hard and learn a lot more than you already have."

"Like what?"

"How to boil dried corn with hardwood ashes to make hominy, for one thing. It's not easy. If you don't do it right, the corn is ruined."

"I'll learn," I answered. "I learned how to milk the goats," I reminded him.

"New dippers need to be carved from gourds," he continued.

"I'll do it."

When Tsan was quiet, I asked, "What else?"

"I have to think," he answered. I handed him the bag of candies.

"What's this?" he demanded.

"Something to eat while you're thinking," I said.

"*Wa tó,*" Tsan answered gruffly. "It would have been easier for you if you'd gone with your aunt, you know. I don't have the things she has."

"No, you don't," I agreed. "But I like it better here. So I'm glad I'm staying."

Tsan held out the bag of candy to me. We each took a piece. "*Ó sta tsi ki*—good," he said.

"*Ó sta tsi ki,*" I confirmed.

"Dorothy Standingdeer came by today, but I told her you went to see your aunt. She said she would come back tomorrow."

"Oh, good. I hope she does—I really want to be friends."

"I think you will," Tsan said. As we walked on, Tsan, having had time to think about it, continued the list of jobs I'd need to perform. "You'll have to make soap, and the mattresses need fresh stuffing. The honey locust tree seed pods will need to be gathered too. Do you know how to tell the honey locust tree?" he asked.

"No," I said, "but you can show me."

Fifteen

I wasn't the only one in training during that summer on Snowbird Mountain. *Tla nu wa* was too. *Tla nu wa* was what Tsan named the eaglet. He said it was the name of a great mythical hawk and that such a fine name would inspire the young bird's spirit. But Father Paul said the silly-looking fledgling was just a big baby, and Baby was the name that stuck.

The most important thing Baby had to learn was how to fly. Tsan explained that in its treetop aerie eaglets begin by jumping about in the nest. Next, they flap their wings and manage to hold themselves airborne for a few seconds at a time while gripping a stick in their talons. This practice prepares the youngsters for successfully gripping a perch. Eagles, Tsan said, fly like hang gliders, so they need a lot of room to spread their wings during takeoffs. Learning to land properly—grabbing on to a high limb with lots of open space around it so it will be easy to take off again—is a key part of learning to fly.

Our fledgling no longer had a nest, though, so as soon as Baby's flight feathers were all in, Tsan and I took turns several times a day coaxing the big youngster onto a stick. We'd bounce this fake branch up and down, and complaining all the while with plaintive peeps, Baby would tightly grip the stick in her talons and flap her wings. The trick was to avoid being whapped in the face by a wing. And it was also smart to keep an eye on Baby's talons—especially once she started lifting off, hovering over the stick for a few seconds, and then settling back down. She was likely to snag your fingers with one of those needle-sharp talons as she reached for the perch and struggled to regain her balance.

When Baby began to improve her grasping and perching skills, Tsan nailed more branches onto her perching stand, including one large limb that had to be braced with a pole to keep it from pulling the whole contraption over. Baby seemed to appreciate his efforts and spent a lot of time hopping along this limb. Tsan said she was learning the art of branch walking.

One thing I learned from Baby was how to "talk" eagle. There was no mistaking her welcoming whistle or the *"kek-kek-kek"* that was her alarm cry. Big as she was, Baby also still made her shrill infant peeps. Tsan taught me how to whistle the way parent eagles do to signal that food is coming. When either of us made this sound, Baby would hunker down, folding her broad wings tightly against her body, and peep. This was her begging display and, instinctively, she wouldn't accept food from us unless we went through this act with her.

With her new sleek black feathers, Baby looked like an adult bird, although her plummage was entirely dark. Tsan explained that it would be several years before the eaglet developed the characteristic white head and tail feathers. She still needed to become more coordinated too. To provide more opportunity to practice taking off and landing, Tsan built a second perch, which he anchored firmly in the ground by piling stones around it. At first, we used fish to coax Baby to fly from perch to perch, but she soon got the idea. In fact, she seemed as eager as we were anxious for her to master this new skill.

To keep Baby supplied with the tremendous quantity of fish she needed, I spent most afternoons fishing. I didn't mind because Dorothy usually came along. While I fished, she sat on the boulder beside me weaving baskets from long, thin white oak splits that she'd soaked in the stream until they were flexible. She told me that her grandmother's fingers were too stiff to weave the strips tightly enough and new baskets were needed to store corn and shell beans for winter.

One basket that she took special care with, Dorothy reported with a wink, would be set aside for the time when she and Calhoun were married. When Dorothy discovered that I not only didn't have any baskets for my future home but that I didn't know how to weave, she was shocked. That night, she came over after supper, bringing oak just right for splitting. As I sat on the floor trying to create oak splits, I began to appreciate the ease with which my friend accomplished this task. I broke more splits than I finished, as I worked to shave and scrape the wood to just the right thinness and smoothness.

"*Ani: yo: wa ne: ka* are so foolish," Dorothy announced as she placed her fingers over mine, guiding the knife blade against the oak split. "They think that the old skills are something to be scorned and forgotten. Then they come to the Qualla Arts and Crafts building and pay high prices for things they should know how to make for themselves."

"Hmm," Tsan agreed as he settled into the rocker by the fireplace and set it into motion. "The old stories must not be lost either."

Dorothy gave me a wink. "Do you know one to teach us, so we can someday share it with our grandchildren?" she asked.

Tsan seemed to ponder this, the creaking of his rocker filling the silence. "Ah, there is a wonderful old tale you should know," he announced at last.

Nv?ya, who was stretched out at Tsan's feet, lifted his head and barked. "He wants a story too," I said as the German shepherd thrust his nose under my hand to let me know he wanted me to scratch behind his ears.

"You won't want to listen to this one, Tla nu wa?" Tsan announced. "Your ancestor is not the hero of this story for once."

"*Kek-kek-kek,*" the eaglet complained, and we all laughed. Then Tsan began the story.

"In the beginning, the world was as cold as the most frigid winter that ever was—colder even. So feathers and fur weren't enough to keep our animal brothers warm. Finally, taking pity on them, the Thunders that live in the clouds sent lightning to put fire into an old sycamore tree growing on an island. Remember how to tell a sycamore tree, Kate?" he asked, pausing.

"You don't know the sycamore tree?" Dorothy asked.

"I *know* it," I said. "A sycamore has giant leaves that

look like this." I traced the shape in the air with my index finger. "And its trunk is silver-white and green and peely."

"Mmm," Tsan agreed. "And down deep in the bottom of a hollow spot in the old sycamore, lightning placed its red-hot fire. The animals saw the lightning come. They knew the fire was in that hollow spot because they could see the smoke coming out. And they wanted that fire the Thunders had sent to warm them. But they couldn't get to the tree because it was on an island surrounded by water. So they held a council to decide what to do."

"What did they decide?" I asked, and Nv?ya licked my arm to remind me of my job.

"Ah, well, it was quite a debate, I can tell you. Every animal that could swim or fly had a different idea of how the fire should be retrieved and who should be the one to do it. After all, the one who would bring the fire to the animals was bound to become a great hero."

"Absolutely," Dorothy agreed. "So who did it?"

"The council finally decided that the raven should have the honor."

"The raven?" I moaned. "That ugly black bird?"

"The raven was quite a different bird in those days," Tsan explained, "not even black, and he was chosen because he was big and strong. So the raven flew across the water and landed on the sycamore tree. But the raven had gone without a plan, and now he wasn't sure how to go about getting the fire out of the deep hollow."

"Figures." I laughed, and the eaglet echoed me with its high-pitched shrieks, as though it agreed with my sentiment.

"Yes, and while that silly bird was sitting on the sycamore wondering what to do, the heat from the fire scorched all its feathers black. This so frightened the raven that it flew back without the fire."

"So I hope the animals picked somebody wiser the next time," Dorothy said.

"They chose the screech owl," Tsan continued. "It planned to fly straight down into the tree. But when it looked down into the hollow, a blast of hot air shot out the hole and nearly burned out the little owl's eyes. It left at once and had a very hard time getting home."

"That's awful," Dorothy said.

"To this day *wa hu hu*'s eyes are red. The horned owl tried next, but the fire nearly blinded that bird as well, and the ashes made white rings around its eyes. It too had to go home without the fire, and no amount of rubbing could get rid of the white rings."

"If the owls weren't able to get the fire out of the hollow in the sycamore tree, what bird could?" I wondered out loud.

"No bird," Tsan said. "Next, the council sent a snake— the black racer. Only, that snake wasn't any blacker than the raven had been in the beginning of the world. The snake swam across to the island, slithered through the grass to the tree, and slipped right into a hole at the bottom of the hollow tree. The animals who were watching all cheered because they felt sure the snake would succeed in retrieving the fire for them. But the smoke and hot ashes were too much for the black racer. After dodging around blindly, he managed only by luck to find his way out. He was scorched black when he returned from the island. And he didn't have the fire."

"So who's left to go after it?" I asked.

"That's what all the animals were wondering," Tsan

said. "They held another council, trying to convince someone to try. But now all the birds, snakes, and four-footed animals had some excuse for why they couldn't possibly go. The truth, of course, was that they were all afraid.

"At last, the water spider volunteered to go. She was able to run on top of the water, so she'd be able to get to the island easily enough, but how would she bring back the fire?

"The animals worried and fussed, offering suggestions about what she should do, but the spider ignored them all. While they argued over what plan might work, she spun a long silken thread and wove it into a bowl-shaped basket. Next, she put this basket on her back. Then she walked across to the island, reached into the tree hollow, and took out one little coal of fire that she put into the basket on her back. Finally, she returned to the animals.

"At last there was a spark with which to light a fire. The animals rejoiced and praised the little water spider. She was very modest about what she'd done, but she did keep her web basket to remind everyone of what she had accomplished."

"So we have a little spider to thank for being warm on a chilly night," I said.

Although I felt certain she'd heard the story before, Dorothy thanked Tsan for sharing it before she left. Tsan in return encouraged Dorothy to come again soon. And so the three of us were together the very next afternoon when the big event finally happened. Baby made her first flight.

None of us actually saw the eaglet take off. We were sitting on the porch. Dorothy was shelling corn, and

Tsan was helping me make the pattern for my rabbit-skin moccasins when Nv?ya started barking frantically. We looked up as the German shepherd sprang from the porch and bounded into the clearing in front of the cabin. Amid excited barks, the big dog leapt into the air, dropped back, and catapulted up again. Baby swooped down in mock combat, her talons barely missing Nv?ya's nose, then her gliding flight carried her soaring up again.

"She's flying. Look! Baby's really *flying*," I shouted.

"*Ó sta tsi ki*," Tsan shouted. "*Ó sta tsi ki.*"

"She looks wonderful!" Dorothy exclaimed.

With one last bark, Nv?ya lapsed into silence and sat down on his haunches with his head still canted skyward. Tsan, Dorothy, and I were now standing in the clearing beside the dog, shading our eyes, and staring into the sky too. As we earthbound admirers watched, the new flier rode a current of air, spiraling higher and higher. And then my joy at seeing the fledgling fly was suddenly replaced by sadness.

"Is Baby leaving?" I asked. She was almost out of sight.

"Yes and no," Tsan replied. "She'll be back, expecting to be fed for another few weeks while she learns to find food for herself. But it won't be long before she begins to wander, heading south to where the waters remain ice-free and she can fish during the long winter months."

"I miss her already," I said.

"It's as it should be," Tsan told me. "Eagles belong to the sky. They are ..." He didn't finish. His expression suddenly became ominous, and he muttered something in Cherokee under his breath.

"What?" I asked. I tilted my head toward the sky

again, squinting against the sun, trying to see what had upset him.

"There," Dorothy said pointing.

A small, silver-white plane gleamed like a jewel set against the faded late afternoon sky. I could hear its engine now, rumbling low like distant thunder. I knew even before the plane began its gliding descent that this was the poachers returning.

Tsan swung around covering the distance to the cabin with purposeful strides. I called after him as he disappeared inside. Nv?ya was on his feet, watching the cabin now. His tail fanned the air in excited anticipation as he pranced forward. Dorothy and I started toward the cabin in Tsan's wake, but before we even reached the porch, Tsan emerged, shoving shells into the open barrel of a shotgun.

"What are you doing?" Dorothy demanded as he charged past us.

"You can't go after them," I insisted.

Tsan stopped and swung back toward Dorothy and me as he jerked the shotgun barrel up, locking it in place with a loud click. "Take Kate to your grandfather's," he said to Dorothy. "Stay there until I come for you," he told me.

"No. I'm coming with you," I said, and Dorothy grabbed my arm to restrain me even though I hadn't yet taken a step.

"Go with Dorothy. *No: kwa*—now!" Tsan repeated. His black eyes seemed to bore into me, but I met his hard gaze evenly. We glared at each other in a silent battle of wills.

Then in a gentle tone, Tsan added, "You must do this for me."

I hesitated several seconds longer before reluctantly

answering, "*Ha yu*—yes, sir." Tsan's expression softened, and the corners of his mouth tugged the tight thin line of his mouth up into a smile—a real smile.

"I'm glad you came to the Snowbirds, Kate," he told me. Then he called to Nv?ya and strode away with the German shepherd close on his heels.

I stood cemented to that spot in the center of the clearing, staring at the forest where Tsan and Nv?ya had disappeared. I felt hot tears well up in my eyes and spill down my cheeks. I wanted to run after them. I was afraid of what might happen to Tsan. Afraid I might lose him too.

I swiped the tears away from my cheeks with my hands as I glared up at the sky. I wished that plane had never come back. I wished Baby would come back so I'd at least know she was safe.

Dorothy squeezed my arm reassuringly.

"Okay," I said, "if we're going, I want to take a few things with me." Dorothy came with me into the cabin while I got my duffel from under Tsan's bed and slipped on my windbreaker.

"Hurry," Dorothy urged.

I was on my way to the door when I hesitated. We didn't have a weapon. I thought about Tsan's rifle but decided taking it didn't make sense. I had never loaded it myself, and I'd only shot it once with Tsan's guidance. On impulse, I picked up the small hand axe that I used to split the chopped wood into chunks just the right size for the stove. This was a tool—weapon— that I definitely had experience using. I tucked the axe into my duffel, feeling more secure.

I reached the door, then hesitated again, and this time Dorothy bumped into me.

"What's wrong?" she demanded.

"What if somebody's out there?"

Still hidden by the deep shadows inside the cabin, I peered out. The clearing to the woods was empty. I held my breath, listening so hard it nearly hurt. I didn't hear anything but familiar sounds—the chickens cackling, the wind stirring the trees, a cicada's drumming. Taking a deep breath, I nodded to Dorothy to follow me. Together, we hurried down the steps, across the clearing, and into the cover of the woods. We didn't head for the ridge this time. Dorothy and I agreed that it would be safer to go around through the woods so we could stay under cover.

We were just below the cave entrance when I heard the eagle's high-pitched cry. *"Kee-yi-yi. Kee-yi-yi."* I looked up, shading my eyes and squinting to see through the fiery haze of the setting sun.

I couldn't see the eaglet, but I heard her cry again. It was Baby. I knew it was.

Baby would probably return to the cabin from her first flight. I pictured her settling onto her perch in the clearing, calling for us, expecting us to deliver her dinner as we had so faithfully until now.

What if the poachers came to the cabin? Baby wouldn't understand that they were dangerous. We'd taught her to trust people. Those men could capture her—easily!

I remembered the black bag writhing as the man lifted it aboard the plane. And I heard Father Paul saying, *"It's all very cruel."* I couldn't take a chance that the poachers would find the eaglet.

"I've got to go back for Baby," I said.

"No, it isn't safe," Dorothy insisted.

"Wait for me here. I'll hurry," I promised, and before Dorothy could stop me, I was off.

A little way down the trail, I thought how much smarter it would have been to have given my duffel bag to Dorothy. But I didn't want to take the time to go back. And I didn't want to just leave the bag out here in the woods in case one of the poachers was scouting around and happened to spot it.

I burst into the clearing at the cabin and saw Baby sitting on her perch—exactly as I'd suspected she'd be. She whistled a greeting when she saw me.

"Pretty proud of yourself, aren't you? Well, you should be!" I beamed. "Baby, you were wonderful, soaring ... like ... like an eagle!"

I was right in front of the eaglet now, and I whistled, wanting her to hunker down as I knew she would in her instinctive feeding display. We had rarely handled Baby because Tsan believed we shouldn't if she was to remain a free spirit. Now I needed her to allow me to touch her, though. I wanted to put her in the cage and carry her—as awkward and difficult as that might be—to So-quah's house.

I set the duffel bag down at my feet and whistled again. Baby began to peep, as she folded her giant wings and lowered her body so her breast feathers spread over the tops of her taloned feet.

"Good, Baby," I crooned as I reached out and placed one hand gently on either side of her body. Her sleek feathers felt as silky as a cat's coat. I began to lift her, and at first she resisted releasing her perch. Then, with even more plaintive peeps than usual, she let go and allowed me to lift her. She was surprisingly light, despite her large size, and I was able to hold her easily.

"I'll find a treat for you," I promised. "You're not going to like it, but I'm going to have to put you back in that cage. Just for a little while." I turned slowly, holding the eaglet gently but firmly cradled in my arms, watching her as I walked toward the cabin. When I sensed I was approaching the steps, I looked up and then stopped short with a startled gasp.

There was a tall, blond, white man standing on the porch. He was smiling, but he definitely didn't look friendly. Especially since he had the muzzle of a shiny silver handgun pointed at my chest.

Sixteen

"Well, well, well. What have we here?" The man's voice rattled deep in his throat. "An eagle? A fine-looking young one. And it's as tame as a kitten. I won't even have to knock that one out of a tree with a tranquilizer gun. We've only got orders for hawks and falcons this time, but I'll bet we can find somebody who wants that bird. There's always somebody who wants eagles."

I was breathing hard, trying to think of what to do, trying not to panic over the gun leveled at my chest. This man was a hulk, tall with bulging arm muscles and a neck so thick he almost appeared not to have a neck at all. The white tips of his small, even teeth peeked from between his lips, making him look as though he were constantly snarling.

Baby still hadn't moved, and the man seemed impressed. "You've really got a way with that bird, kid." With his free hand he pulled a black bag out of his jacket pocket. "How's about I hold this and you just stuff that eagle on in here?"

He began walking down the steps toward me, and I still didn't move. My attention was riveted on the gun coming closer. Then the man was directly in front of me.

"Okay, kid," he said. "Do it. Now."

I didn't plan what happened next. It was fear and reflex that made me suddenly jerk my arms up and toss Baby at the man's face. I saw the eaglet's feet thrust forward. I could only guess where the sharp taloned toes struck, because Baby's flailing wings hid the man's face. But I knew they'd snagged flesh from the way the man was screaming.

"Get out of here, Baby," I shouted. Probably more from her own instinct than my command, the young eagle flapped harder and lifted into the air. I had one quick glimpse of blood spurting between fingers as the man crumpled like a deflated toy with his hands pressed to his face. I spotted the gun then, where it had dropped at the man's feet, and stooped to retrieve it.

Just as my fingers closed around the gun's handle, the man's hand jerked away from his mangled face and snagged my wrist. I screamed, struggling to pull free. But the man's fingers were a handcuff anchoring me to him. The eaglet's talons had only gouged his cheeks and forehead, which made him lucky in a way. It also made him hideous and furious. The man's ice-blue eyes glared at me from the puffy, bloody mask of his face. I shrieked again and again in fear as I tugged and writhed.

"*Kek-kek-kek!*" This shrill cry heralded Baby's swooping dive. I felt the brush of her wing tip as her talons raked the top of the man's blond head. And his hand instantly released me as he flung his arms up to protect himself. I scrambled to my feet—still holding the gun—and ran.

I charged into the woods, dodging around trees, leaping fallen logs, running full out. Then my toe caught a root, and I crashed forward, scraping my cheek on a rough tree trunk, landing so hard that my hands dug divots into the soft ground. The gun jerked out of my hand and skipped like a flat stone hopping across a lake.

Fresh panic flooded through me as I clawed at the ground, struggling to get back on my feet as quickly as possible. I snatched up the gun and ran on.

I didn't glance behind me until I heard the man's curses. He'd fallen, too, and when I looked, he was pulling on a tree limb to get back on his feet. "I'll get you, you little wretch!" he bellowed when, for a fleeting instant, our eyes met.

I turned and fled again. This time I made more of an effort to watch where I was going and to avoid tripping over roots. It wasn't easy, though, because I was running so hard.

I reached the stream at a spot where the bank was really steep. I thought about following the stream until I found an easier spot to cross, but I could hear the man pushing through the brush—coming closer. I sat and slid down the muddy slope.

When my feet hit the icy water, I jumped up and waded across. I was climbing up the bank on the opposite side when the man chasing me bounded down the slope and into the stream.

"Now I've got you," he yelled, and I scrambled harder.

But it was a lot more difficult to go up a steep, muddy bank than to go down. I was frantic, knowing how close the man was to reaching me.

I was almost to the top when he lunged for me. I heaved myself up onto the grassy crest of the slope just as the man slipped. Cursing, he seemed to recover and started forward again. Then, wildly waving his arms, he went over backward. A plume of water jetted out from either side as he flopped down, spewing more curses.

This was my chance, and getting back on my feet, I started running away from the stream. But I had taken only a few strides when another man stepped out from behind a tree to block my path. He was a medium-size man with closely cropped brown hair and a pencil-thin mustache, wearing camouflage-colored hunting coveralls and dark glasses.

"What the hell's going on?" he demanded, not of me but of my dripping wet pursuer. The blond-haired man had crawled out of the stream on all fours and was now rising slowly like a grizzly bear rearing to attack.

Remembering the gun in my hand, I raised my arm, taking a shaky aim at the new man's chest. "Don't come any closer or I'll shoot," I stammered.

"Christ, Houston! You let this girl get your gun," the man moaned. Then, as though he'd just noticed, he added, "What happened to your face?"

"Stay right there or I'll shoot," I announced, swinging my aim toward the blond-haired man.

"Girly, you aren't going to blow away anybody but yourself if you pull the trigger with all that crap in your gun barrel," the man in coveralls told me.

I looked down at the weapon in my hand, appalled to discover brown gunk dripping from the silver barrel. The man snatched the muddy gun from my hand and shoved it into one of the deep pockets of his hunting suit.

"An eagle got me. That kid was holding it," Houston reported in childlike agony. "And she threw it at me. I'm gonna break her little neck." He took a step toward me and a lightning flash of fresh fear shivered through my entire body.

"Later," the man who'd taken my gun snapped.

"Look what she done to me, Mac!" Houston stormed. "I'm gonna ..."

"Later, I said," Mac repeated. "Craig isn't going to want to take off from that field once it's dark, and this deal is r-u-s-h. If we want that bonus, we've got to collect the birds and get back to Atlanta in time to meet our transport. We can take these two locals along in the plane and deal with them at our leisure once this mission's over."

"Mission?" Houston laughed, and the grin looked strange amid his swollen, bloody features. "Mac, you sound like you're still in the marines."

"Yeah, well there's nothing wrong with that, is there?" Mac grumbled, grabbing my arm and yanking me along in his wake. "I still would be a marine if some jackass colonel hadn't had me court-martialed."

I tried to keep pace, but I couldn't seem to move fast enough to suit the ex-marine. He slapped me hard, telling me to quit trying to be a "dead weight." Houston guffawed loudly at this.

I tried harder to keep up and to pay attention so I didn't stumble, but I couldn't stop thinking about Mac's words. He'd said he would *take care of both of us*. Did that mean the poachers had already captured Tsan? Or maybe Dorothy?

We reached the meadow where the plane was parked. Mac marched me over to the open cargo door and told me to get in. As I climbed into the plane I saw Tsan with his arms bound behind his back and his feet tied together. He was lying on his side with his back to me.

"You've killed him," I shrieked, hurrying to Tsan.

"Naw," Houston growled. "He's just sleeping."

I saw the tranquilizer darts then—one in his hip and one sticking out of his chest. "You shot him *twice*," I said accusingly, plucking out the darts.

"He was tough to bring down." Houston seemed offended by my comment, and I suspected he was the one who had done the shooting. "The old coot thought he was a warrior buck, sniping at us until I got around behind him." I could imagine that scene, and my heart went out to Tsan. I leaned over him, loosening the collar of his plaid flannel shirt, patting his cheek, trying to revive him.

"Enough!" Mac snapped. "Tie her up and let's go hunting. If Craig bags all the birds by himself, he won't give us a share of the bonus."

That threat seemed to be the motivation Houston needed. He quickly climbed into the plane and pulled me away from Tsan. Taking a long yellow nylon rope from a supply bag, he tied my wrists together behind my back. Then he made me sit down, bound my ankles, threaded the rope once more behind me, and secured the end with a knot between my wrists.

"There. A nice little package. Don't go away," he

added, flicking my chin so hard that my head jerked up. Then Houston slipped out of the plane, and he and Mac disappeared from view.

I stayed perfectly still, listening hard, until I was sure they had really gone. Then I began to try to tug my hands out of their noose. "Tsan," I called, struggling to loosen the rope. "Tsan, you've got to wake up." There was no response, and I wiggled across the plane's floor until I was next to him. I leaned against him, patting his back with my fingers. "Tsan. Please hear me."

Finally, he groaned. "Tsan. Oh, yes. C'mon. Wake up. It's me Kate. Tsan." I slapped my bound hand against his back. "C'mon. Please."

Tsan rolled toward me, licking his lips. His eyes opened a crack. Then he coughed. "What?" He coughed again. "How did they find you? Where's Dorothy?"

"She's all right ... I think. I went back to the cabin for Baby," I admitted. "I heard her call and I was afraid the poachers would get her."

"Yes," Tsan said in a tone that said he approved of my actions despite the consequences.

"Baby got one of those poachers, though. You should have seen her ..." I was about to tell him more about what had happened when Tsan shushed me. I'd heard the sound too. Could the poachers be returning already?

Suddenly Nv?ya jumped through the cargo door. The big German shepherd bounded over to lap my face in a cheerful greeting.

"Nv?ya, come here," Tsan ordered, but the dog had already jumped out through the cargo door again.

"Nv?ya?" I called.

"Where'd he go?" Tsan demanded. The dog returned then, but this time it was obviously hard for him to pull himself through the cargo door. The German shepherd was working hard to tug something in with him.

"My duffel bag!" I exclaimed when I caught a glimpse of Nv?ya's burden.

"Fool dog," Tsan muttered.

"No. Wonderful, wonderful dog," I announced. "He must have gone back to the cabin and found it in the clearing where I left it. Bring the bag here, Nv?ya. Oh, good dog." The big dog obeyed, pulling the duffel within reach of my bound hands.

"What good is that?" Tsan demanded groggily.

My fingers had managed to grasp the zipper pull, and I worked it open slowly. "I have the small axe," I explained.

"Yes, that will cut this rope," Tsan agreed. He rolled over so that his bound hands were toward me. "Hold the blade steady, and I will use the sharp edge to cut the rope binding my wrists together."

"I don't have the axe yet," I told him. I'd managed to open the zipper, but I was having trouble searching for the axe. I found that pulling my legs up tightly against my chest gave me a little slack to move my hands more freely.

"There." My fingers touched the sharp edge of the blade. "I found it."

"Get it out of the bag."

"I'm trying. I'm trying. There. Okay, I'm holding it now." I squirmed to bring the axe closer to Tsan. "Try to get even closer," I said. We were both puffing from our struggles.

Finally, Tsan positioned his hands so that one was on

either side of the axe and the rope was stretched over the sharp blade. "Now, hold tight," he instructed. Tsan sawed his hands back and forth, bumping me with each stroke, so that keeping the axe blade in an upright position was difficult.

"A little more," Tsan grunted. "A ... little ... more." Tsan's hands broke free with a thunk, and he took the axe from me. With quick skillful strokes, he finished freeing himself. Then he cut the rope binding my hands. I pulled the yellow cord until it loosened enough to slide off my ankles.

"Hurry," Tsan said as he helped me out through the cargo door. I looked back up at him still standing in the plane door. "Don't go back to the cabin for any reason this time," he ordered. "And be careful."

"Aren't you coming with me?"

"I'll follow soon," Tsan promised. "Now, please obey me. For once," he added. Then he disappeared back into the shadowy darkness of the cargo hold. Doing as I'd been told, I turned toward the woods and ran.

Long shadows stretched out from the tall trees and striped the ground. I sped across them, feeling as if I were leaping from one shadow to the next. Nv?ya loped along beside me, running so close that his warm furry body occasionally brushed against me. I wondered if Dorothy had escaped from the woods. I prayed she was safe at her grandparents'.

Nv?ya and I reached the stream quickly and followed the winding water course to my usual fishing spot. There was barely any bank here. I started for the water, but Nv?ya hesitated, whimpering.

When none of my coaxing persuaded him to follow me, I grabbed the scruff of his neck like a big puppy and tugged him into the water. The stream was colder now since the afternoon's warmth was slipping away with the light, and I was frustrated when Nv?ya stopped midstream. No amount of tugging would budge the big dog an inch farther.

"C'mon, Nv?ya," I pleaded. "Please. I'm freezing to death." The German shepherd's neck stretched forward in response to my tugs but his feet remained firmly anchored.

"Nv?ya! Please. I know you're worried about Tsan, but he wants us to be safe. Come on." I gave an extra hard tug to punctuate my command and Nv?ya stopped resisting. True to Newton's Law, as the German shepherd sprang forward, I flopped backward.

"Oh, Nv?ya," I groaned, sinking into the icy cold stream. I got up, dripping, and made my way out of the water to the bank where the dog sat watching me with his big brown eyes as though asking what had taken me so long.

"N-now I really am freez-ing to death," I stammered as my teeth started to chatter uncontrollably. Nv?ya's response was to block my way, baring his teeth threateningly.

"Hey, what's the matter with you? How come I'm suddenly the enemy again?"

Nv?ya persisted in holding me at bay. When I tried to walk around him, he bounded ahead of me. Then he planted himself in front of me again and growled a throaty warning to stop. Eventually, the dog backed me into a giant rhododendron bush, and I sank to the ground beside it.

"Okay. Okay. You win," I announced. "I don't understand why you're doing this, but you win." As though to apologize for his actions, Nv?ya lay down beside me and plopped his big head onto my lap.

I snuggled against the dog's warm body, shivering, and began stroking his neck. "You're nuts," I whispered into one of his velvety ears.

Then I felt the German shepherd tense, and the ear next to my mouth twitched. I straightened, listening, and I heard a sharp snap. Someone—not very far away—had just stepped on a branch.

Seventeen

K-A-B-O-O-M! The explosion made me forget about everything else—about being wet and cold, about being afraid that one of the poachers was nearby. I forgot about everything—except Tsan.

K-A-B-O-O-M! I leapt to my feet as the second explosion shuddered through me. I could see a fireball where I knew the meadow was. Where I knew the plane was. Where I had left Tsan. I watched the thick inky-black smoke boil up from the flames, painting a more intense blackness across the already darkening sky.

Oh, please, let Tsan be all right, I thought.

"It's the plane!" shouted a voice too close. Startled, I turned toward that sound and, by chance, looked straight into Mac's eyes. The three poachers, carrying four bulging black bags between them, weren't a dozen yards away from me on the other side of the rhododendron bush.

"They got away," announced one man whom I hadn't seen before. He was a black man about as tall as Houston, although skinny by comparison, and dressed all in black—a black turtleneck knit shirt and black slacks.

We stood staring at each other, the poachers and I, for a second or two, maybe longer. Then a third explosion broke the spell. The black man shouted something about his plane. He and Mac took off, running toward the stream and heading for the blazing meadow.

"You shoulda let me take care of her earlier," Houston fumed, following the ex-marine. "Shoulda let me finish off both of 'em."

Mac stopped at the stream's edge and pivoted so suddenly that the big blond man couldn't avoid colliding with him. "Get her now," Mac roared, pointing at me.

It was obvious that no command could have pleased Houston more. A murderous grin split the puffy mask of the blond man's wounded face. Then he shoved the single bag he was carrying into Mac's hands and hurled himself across the space that separated us.

I sidestepped, just barely managing to elude Houston's huge hands, as he grabbed for me across the rhododendron bush. Nv?ya growled and leapt, sinking his teeth into the big man's forearm, but Houston shook him off as if he were just a toy dog. The German shepherd rolled when he landed and was instantly on his feet again, charging back to do battle.

As I ran along the stream's edge I picked up stones and hurled them at the big blond man. "That's for shooting my grandfather with a tranquilizer gun," I shouted, pelting Houston and diving after more rocks.

"That's for Baby. And that's for ..." But Houston was like a tank—powerful and unstoppable. Without seeming to care that the German shepherd had chomped onto his leg, this hulk of a man stomped over to me and grabbed my arm midswing.

"Gotcha!" His horrible grin was just inches from my face now.

I knew that shoving your knee into a man's groin is supposed to be an effective way to escape, but I wasn't sure I could hit this man hard enough to do more than just make him angrier. Instead, I took the smooth, round water-polished stone in my free hand and smashed it into his swollen cheek.

The big blond man yowled and let go of me. This was exactly the effect I'd hoped for, and encouraged by my success, I decided to try a kick after all. The yowl became a howl as my foot connected between Houston's legs, and the hulk sank to his knees.

Finally, I picked up one more large rock with both hands and brought it down—hard—on top of Houston's blond head. There was a hollow thunk as the rock hit, and the big man flopped forward, sprawling on the ground.

"One down!" I announced, tossing the stone into the stream, where it landed with a splash. "Now, let's get out of here, Nv?ya."

"Hold it right there," Mac growled. He was standing on the opposite side of the stream. He wasn't holding any of the black bags now. Instead, he had a handgun, and it wasn't the muddy one.

"You and that old Indian live somewhere around here, don't you?" he demanded as he came across the stream toward me. I was still in shock from his sudden arrival and didn't answer fast enough to suit him. Mac's slap nearly knocked me off my feet. Nv?ya instantly leapt to my defense, and Mac smashed the gun's handle into the German shepherd's skull. The big dog fell to the ground, a furry heap at my feet.

"Nv?ya," I gasped. I started to bend over the dog, but Mac grabbed my arm and jerked me upright.

"That old man blew up my plane, and now I've got to get off this mountain. I want his car." The ex-marine's fingers dug fiercely into my arm.

"We don't have a car," I stammered.

"A Jeep then. Or a truck," Mac snapped.

"No. No Jeep. No truck."

"Liar!" Mac slapped me again.

I was not quite sure what happened next because so many things seemed to happen all at once. It might have been Nv?ya regaining consciousness and biting Mac's ankle. Or it might have been Tsan bursting from the bushes and jumping Mac. Or it might even have been Houston dragging his hulking frame back up on to his feet again with a groan. Whatever triggered it, the result was a free-for-all battle with everyone swinging and kicking, ducking, getting knocked down, and getting up again.

I couldn't tell if my side was winning or losing. We definitely seemed to be holding our own. Then suddenly, Tsan broke free and grabbed my hand, shouting for me to run. Together we made a dash for the cabin.

"I've got to get my rifle. Then I can hold them off," Tsan told me as we ran up the porch steps and charged through the door. I slammed the door behind Nv?ya and shoved the rocker against it with the back under the knob.

"You've got to put a lock on this door," I reported.

"Gone," Tsan announced.

"What?" I asked.

"My rifle."

"That big blond man—Houston—was here," I told him. "Before, when I came back to the cabin for Baby, he was on the porch. He didn't have the rifle, though—just a pistol."

"Then he must have done something with the rifle." Tsan frowned.

"What'll we do now?" I asked. But there wasn't time for an answer. Nv?ya growled a deep rumbling alert that danger was approaching.

The sharp burst of the shotgun's blast split the air at the same instant that the window closest to me shattered, showering me with glass fragments. I shrieked, and Tsan was instantly beside me, pushing me to the floor. "Stay down," he said, just as a whole volley of gunfire rang out, shattering the other window and spraying splinters. Nv?ya was beside me too. I covered the dog's eyes with my hands and buried my face in his soft shoulder.

"Come out of there, or we'll come in after you." I recognized Houston's voice.

Belly crawling across the glass-strewn floor, Tsan got his hunting knife from where it hung in a leather sheath on a peg next to the door. He stayed crouched behind the door, but no one charged us. In fact, everything suddenly seemed very quiet. Too quiet.

"What's going on?" I whispered, caressing Nv?ya's head as much to comfort myself as the dog. Tsan only shrugged, indicating that he didn't know.

"Did you really blow up their plane?" I asked.

"Yes," Tsan answered softly. "I wanted to stop them from taking the birds away." He cast me a sad smile that showed he felt the irony of this, since now he obviously wished the poachers would leave. "I'm afraid that one man wants revenge," he added.

Tsan meant Mac, of course, but I thought about how I'd managed to get the best of Houston. I suspected he wanted revenge too. Only Craig seemed to have left. Perhaps he was watching over the bagged birds. Suddenly, thumps overhead made me look up at the rough-hewn rafters.

"Hey, old man." Mac's voice came from above us. "Remember that can of kerosene you had out in the shed?"

An oily, brown drop dripped onto my hand. And I smelled the heavy—almost sweet—odor of kerosene. I broke into a cold sweat as I realized that Mac was dousing the roof with it.

"Tsan?" I whispered. But before Tsan could answer me, there was a sort of *"poof,"* followed by a crackling sound like plastic wrap being crumpled. Blue-orange tongues of flame instantly lapped between several of the rafters, and thick, gray tendrils of smoke began to spiral downward.

"C'mon out, girly." Houston laughed. "You, too, old man. C'mon. We're waitin' on you."

"Let 'em burn," Mac growled. "Serve 'em right."

I jumped to my feet in panic. I desperately wanted to flee the blue and orange flames that were spreading across the rafters above my head with surprising swiftness. But Tsan caught my arm with a firm grip.

"No," he ordered. "Wait. They'll shoot us."

"We're trapped," I moaned, starting to cry. Nv?ya began to whimper.

"We've got to stop the fire," Tsan said. He had grabbed a blanket from his bed and was swatting at the fiery tongues. I grabbed another blanket and began beating at the flames flowing down the wall by the fireplace.

We worked frantically, and with each swat another spot of fire disappeared leaving only gray smoke. I felt sure we were winning this battle. Then part of the roof crashed in, showering sparks, and the fire began to spread with alarming speed.

The whole kitchen area was ablaze. Flames flowed across the floor and up over Tsan's bed, then engulfed it, so that the bed appeared to have a fiery orange spread.

"Tsan!" I shouted. He stopped swatting at the flames and turned around, dazed. His expression was one of complete horror. His little cabin that had seemed such a snug, safe place on chilly nights was now a frightening, fiery trap. Where there wasn't fire, there was smoke so thick, gray, and acrid that it seemed too dense to breathe. It made my lungs ache and made it hard to move. The blanket felt as heavy as lead now in my hands, and my arms were wooden limbs too awkward to lift.

Tsan began to do something that seemed too absurd to be real. He was using the old shovel to scoop the fiery logs out of the fireplace and toss them into the room. When the hearth was empty, he reached out to me, pulling me through the thick gray, bitter-tasting smoke into the fireplace beside him. Once I was inside the chimney, I was surprised by a breeze. The cool air blew into my upturned face and washed the smoke from my eyes and nose. I sucked in this deliciously fresh air open-mouthed, gasping as it pushed the smoke out of my lungs.

"Climb, Kate," Tsan insisted, taking the blanket out of my hand.

"Nv?ya," I called. The German shepherd had taken refuge under the table, and he was curled up as he might huddle against a driving snowstorm. I called again, but Nv?ya still didn't respond. Then more of the roof smashed down in a cloud of sparks as brilliant as being inside an exploding skyrocket.

"Climb, Kate," Tsan ordered, giving me a push to start me up the rough clay brick chimney wall. "*U hóh saa—* be strong!" he urged with the *Tsa la ki* warrior cry. And I began to climb, finding chinks into which I could poke my toes and crevices wide enough to hold my fingers.

When I heard more of the roof—or maybe it was a wall this time—collapse, I looked back down the chimney expecting to see Tsan climbing behind me. But he wasn't there.

"Tsan!" I screamed. Only the flames answered, shooting sparks up the chimney. These stung like wasps as they struck my bare hands and cheek. Frightened that my hair might catch on fire, I frantically began climbing again.

Higher. Higher. The sky and freedom were just ahead of me. I could see it as a dark hole at the end of the flame-lit tunnel, and I pulled myself up toward that dark spot as quickly as I could. Panting, calling on my last reserve of energy, I finally drew myself up past the lip of the chimney. I threw one leg over to anchor myself and took a deep breath. Santa had never been more glad to get out of a chimney than I felt in that moment of triumph.

But what had happened to Tsan and Nv?ya? I wondered. And what was going to happen to me now?

I realized suddenly that I hadn't really escaped. There was no way to get down from the roof, which was a sea of flames. I felt like I was sitting atop a rocket ship that was about to take off. There was so much fire around me—there was even a deafening roar like a rocket ship launching.

Then a tremendous wind kicked up. It was so strong that I had to cling to the brick lip of the chimney to keep from being blown away. I thought it was a storm brewing again, and for a second I hoped it might rain hard enough to put out the fire. I suspected that the poachers had abandoned us and fled. But even if they were still around, I decided that I would gladly face them rather than burn to death.

Another strong gust of wind swept the roof as the roar grew even louder. Only this time, I realized that the roar was coming from directly above me. A helicopter was hovering overhead, and two men in helmets and green puffy jackets leaned out. Then a rope ladder descended toward me.

"Grab it!" The shout sounded like a whisper because of the helicopter's noise and wind. Even before the ladder was really close enough, I reached up for it. And as it came closer, I stretched, straining to reach even farther. The ladder seemed to float tantalizingly close. I leaned still farther and nearly lost my balance.

"You can do it!" called a voice. I wanted to do it. I had to reach that rope ladder. I pulled my other leg up onto the chimney lip and pushed myself up into a crouching position.

With a splintering, shattering sound and a fountain of hot, stinging sparks, one whole wall of the blazing cabin crashed inward. The chimney shuddered, and I tottered on my perch. Panic made me crouch lower and cling more tightly.

"C'mon, kid. You can do it." The shouts encouraged me. I swallowed, fighting against the fear that anchored me to this spot. Finally, I pushed myself up higher again.

"That's it. C'mon, kid." This time as the rope ladder danced above my hand, I flung myself at it. I had the same sensation I'd had the first time I ever went off the high dive at the swimming pool. I really wished I hadn't done it, but once I jumped there was no turning back.

I caught the bottom rung of the ladder with a jerk that sliced pain through my entire body.

"Hang on, kid," cheered the voice, as I was yanked off the chimney. The ladder swung crazily first one way and then another.

I felt myself rising. I wasn't sure if it was the helicopter going up or the ladder being pulled up. I finally decided that it was both. I could see the flaming cabin dropping away below me. Then strong hands—several pairs of hands—grabbed my hands, the back of my jacket, and hooked under my arms. I was lifted aboard the helicopter.

Now the helicopter churned away faster. I sat up, pulling my legs up so my knees were under my chin. I was shaking, although I wasn't really cold. One man wrapped a blanket around my shoulders. Another smiled at me and gave me the thumbs-up sign. He wanted me to know that I was okay, but I didn't really feel okay—not without Tsan.

"We have to go back!" I shouted over the roar of the helicopter's engine. "We have to help my grandfather get out!"

"We didn't see anyone else," one of the men shouted back. "There was another chopper ahead of us. They probably got your grandfather out."

I felt the tears well up in my eyes. I hoped the man was right, that another helicopter had rescued Tsan and Nv?ya.

For the whole long ride, all I could do was swallow my tears as images of Tsan and Nv?ya and Dorothy raced through my mind. I was sure that Dorothy must have escaped. But what had happened to my grandfather?

Eighteen

The helicopter landed on a cement strip behind a silvery metal Quonset hut that gleamed in the brightness of the huge search lights. By contrast the night sky overhead looked inky black because the lights made it impossible to distinguish the twinkling stars. Even the nearly full moon looked like a pale spot someone had pasted on a background of sky. The man who had given me the thumbs-up sign jumped out and then helped me down.

"C'mon, honey," he said. "Let's go inside so Doc can take a look at you."

"But you've got to go back," I insisted again, my voice shrill with panic. "My grandfather's still back there."

"I told you, honey," the man said, "I'm sure the other chopper picked up your grandfather."

"But what if they didn't? You *have* to go back," I pleaded. I couldn't stop the tears that were spilling out of my eyes. They made the stark whiteness of the medical hut a dazzling blur as I walked stiffly down the hall with my rescuers.

Then I heard a bark. It was unmistakable and it came from behind the screen at the far end of the hut.

"Nv?ya? Tsan?" I called. Tsan appeared slowly from behind the screen. Both of his hands were swabbed in white bandages that looked like giant mittens. When he saw me, he started toward me, slowly, but I was already running toward him. When I reached Tsan, I threw my arms around his neck, hugging him—hard.

"Oh, Grandfather. When I looked down the chimney and didn't see you, I was so afraid you were ..." I couldn't say it. I couldn't say what I'd been afraid of. And then I realized that I wasn't the only one hugging. Tsan was hugging me back. Tears welled in my eyes and poured freely down my cheeks.

"I couldn't leave Nv?ya," Tsan said. "I wrapped the blanket over both of us and dashed out the door. The men from the helicopter were there. They thought I was one of the poachers at first. I tried to tell them that you were still inside, but they wouldn't listen." There were tears in his dark eyes now, and I hugged him again.

Nv?ya came around the screen then, limping and whimpering for attention. He had three of his four feet bandaged. "Oh, poor Nv?ya," I crooned, stooping to pet the big dog. He lapped my face with a wet tongue, and his bushy tail wagged an enthusiastic welcome.

"There you are. Praise be to God! You're alive," Father Paul said as he came into the room. Dorothy was with him, and she rushed to throw her arms around me.

"I was so scared," she told me. "My grandfather called the Agency about the poachers, but then we saw the smoke."

"Luckily so did the forest ranger," the priest added. "And he called the Air National Guard."

The man in uniform who had been standing at a nearby desk talking on the phone called out, "Good news. The poachers have been captured."

"That's wonderful!" Father Paul exclaimed.

"Oh, but your cabin, Tsan," I cried.

Tsan nodded sadly. "You will need to go to your aunt now, Kate," he told me.

"No," I said with such conviction that everyone looked surprised. "I won't go."

"Kate, you promised," the priest insisted.

"I promised to go to live with her at the end of the summer," I pointed out. "I don't intend to be cheated out of one day of being here. Nothing has to change just because all this happened." Tsan looked stern, and I felt intimidated by him again.

"Couldn't I stay, please?" I asked him. Then I stood very still and held my breath as Tsan's black eyes seemed to bore into me.

When Tsan finally answered, his response was a flat refusal. "I haven't got anything at all to offer you," he said.

"You could love me," I said "I mean do you think you could learn to love me, please, Grandfather, because I already love *you* a lot."

"You would choose to stay with me over going to be with your aunt and uncle, Kate?" Tsan demanded. "You'd choose that even now?"

I knew he was thinking about my father, and I answered without hesitation, "Absolutely!"

Then Tsan opened his arms to me again, and I went into them happily. "*Kv: ke: yu:?*—I love you, Granddaughter," he told me. "But I'm an old man who has grown used to living alone, and now I don't even have a home to offer you."

"There is a solution to that," Father Paul said. "I'll call the parish committee first thing in the morning. We'll organize a work day immediately, and everyone on the Qualla Boundary will pitch in to help you rebuild. You'll have a new home in no time."

"I ... I don't know," Tsan stammered, still hesitating.

"I'll help," Dorothy piped up.

"You can count on me too," announced the guardsman. "I'll see to it that the building supplies get delivered to the site. Just name the day."

"See," Father Paul said. "And maybe your new cabin can even have some modern amenities, like plumbing. You can give Kate a home if you want to, Tsan. In fact, you owe it to her for the rest of the summer. You did agree to that, and I'd say that Kate has more than held up her end of the bargain."

"You did promise," I insisted.

Tsan held up his bandaged hands in surrender. "Kate can stay until the end of the summer," he agreed in his usual gruff tone, but now there was a twinkle in his eyes.

"You folks are welcome to stay here at the infirmary until you build your new cabin," the guardsman offered.

Tsan was explaining that he had goats and chickens and an eagle to tend to when Dorothy Standingdeer's parents arrived, along with Dorothy's older brother and a younger sister. The story had to be retold for their benefit, and when they'd heard what had happened, Dorothy's parents insisted we spend the night with them.

"Tomorrow," Charlie Standingdeer announced, "I'll

drive you up the mountain, and my son and I will build a lean-to where you can stay until your cabin is rebuilt." He paused, then added, "Perhaps Kate would like to stay at our house until the cabin is finished. I'm sure Dorothy would enjoy that."

Dorothy grinned and we hugged each other again. After the doctor dressed my burns, I climbed into the backseat of the Standingdeers' station wagon between Dorothy and her brother. Nv?ya sat between my legs, resting both his head and one bandaged paw on my knee. Perhaps to take all of our minds off what had happened as we rode along the conversation focused on the forthcoming Green Corn Festival. Listening, I realized that, whatever comforts Aunt Mildred and Uncle Frank might be able to provide for me, my life with them would never be half as interesting as what I could experience right here.

I thought about Mom and how happy we'd been together. I knew I would always miss her. Remembering her made me think about the house that had been my home until now. It was full of all my growing-up memories and all of my things—my bed with the white eyelet spread, my posters and stuffed animals, and my art supplies and sketches.

"Tsan," I shouted. "They all burned up."

"What?" Tsan asked, puzzled. The car had stopped in front of the Standingdeers' house, and everyone began to get out.

"Your beautiful sketches," I said. "Oh, I'm so sorry, Grandfather." I began to cry again.

"It's all right, Kate," Tsan put his arm around my shoulders and pulled me against him. "I'll draw more," he promised.

"I like to draw too," I told him. "Maybe we can sketch together."

"*Ó sta tsi ki*—good! I'd like that," he said. "It will give me a chance to show you more of our *Tsa la ki* mountains. There is so much I want to share with you, Granddaughter." Tsan smiled at me and wiped away my tears with his bandaged hands.

"C'mon," Nancy Standingdeer said, inviting us in. "I'm going to get us all something to eat."

"She baked a chocolate pound cake. You haven't tasted anything until you've tasted Nancy's chocolate cake," Charlie Standingdeer said. Then he picked up the limping Nv?ya and carried him into the house. As my grandfather and I followed more slowly, I realized that even without a house, I'd begun to feel that I'd found a home with Tsan, Nv?ya, Baby, and some wonderful new friends.

"You know," I said, "I think you should build a bigger cabin this time so there could be bedrooms—one for you and one for me."

"*Umpf,*" Tsan grunted. I wasn't sure what that meant, but it had sounded positive. Very positive.

Glossary of Cherokee Words and Phrases

1. *Hi hwi lo hi*—instruction to leave or go away
2. *Ke?i hwi lo hi*—instruction to go downstream
3. *No: kwa!*—Now! (a command)
4. *Ta ka no hi:li*—flying in this direction
   U wo ha? li—eagle
   Ti:ye:? stih ski—waking them up
5. *Ata: lo: nu heh ski*—traitor
6. *A yo: wa ne: ka*—white person
   Ani: yo: wa ne: ka—white people
7. *Ayv:wi yá hi*—Indian
8. *Thu: thi*—Snowbird
   Thu? thi: yi—Snowbird Place
9. *Nv: ne hi*—sacred people of the mountain; immortals
10. *U hóh saa*—be strong!
11. *To hi yu*—true

12. *Ta wih ska la*—flint
13. *A nih ski:na*—satanistic spirits
14. *Kho:lan a nih ye: li: ski*—Raven Mockers (evil spirits)
15. *Ata: wé hi*—wizard
16. *Se:lu*—corn
17. *Tsa la ki*—Cherokee
18. *Ó sta tsi ki*—it is good
19. *Kha no: na*—mortar for grinding corn
20. *Ka no he: na*—sour corn gruel
21. *Tho: tsuh wa*—redbird or cardinal
22. *To: yi*—beaver
23. *Ah wi*—deer
24. *Ka: kal ka nv hi ta*—Long Hams (bear)
25. *Tso: la ka yv: li*—ancient tobacco
26. *Koh sv hih sah nv hi–tso: la*—
    remake tobacco to give it magical powers
27. *Wa tó*—thanks!
28. *Wa hu hu*—screech owl
    U: ku? khu—hoot owl.
29. *Kv: ke: yu: ?*—I love you

JESUS LOVES ME
Tsis a:ki ke: yú.

Tsis a:ki ke: yú.
Jesus loves me.
koh wel a:khi no hi se.
Book   It tells me.
Tsu: nah sti ka Tsu: tse: li.
Little Ones   Belong to him.
U: hli ni: ki tih ye: hno.
Because he is strong.

Tsis   *a:ki ke: yú.*
Jesus   Loves me.
Tsis   *a:ki ke: yú.*
Jesus   Loves me.
Tsis   *a:ki ke: yú.*
Jesus   Loves me.
akhi no hih se ho.
He tells me so.

About the Author

SANDRA MARKLE grew up hiking, fishing, swimming, and appreciating nature in the windswept farm country of northern Ohio. Later, she moved to the mountains of North Carolina where she taught in a rural school near Cherokee and visited the Qualla Boundary frequently. "I developed a great admiration for the Cherokee people and I was especially impressed with their sense of community both among each other and with nature. Several years ago I became concerned with the problem of poaching predator birds, which is portrayed in this book. My telling of this story was influenced by my great love for my own grandfather."

Sandra Markle has written numerous books, workbooks, articles, and television programs for young people on science topics. She lives in Atlanta, Georgia, with her husband and two children.